The Good Life

The Good Life

A Chris Garrett Novel

DAVID G. WHITE

HARMON AND WHITE PUBLISHING
NAPA VALLEY, CALIFORNIA

Harmon and White Publishing
1003 Dealy Lane
Napa, CA 94559

Library of Congress Control Number: 2006939044

White, David G., 2007
The Good Life / David G. White

ISBN-13: 978-0-9791583-0-8
ISBN-10: 0-9791583-0-3

Printed in the United States of America

10 9 8 7 6 5 4 3 2 1

This book is printed on acid-free paper.

For Lois: the sweetest part.

The Good Life

Chapter
1

I AWOKE WITH a start. Somebody was banging on my front door, really hammering on it and had been for some time. From the pounding, I suspected the only way I was ever getting back to sleep was if I got up and answered it, so I did. I threw off the covers and navigated my way though the apartment with eyes mostly shut and mind still in a fog. I also suspected it was still early, much too early from the light or rather lack of light that was streaming in from the windows to be woken up in such a manner.

At the front door through the glass I saw the culprit; it was Marjorie, my landlady. I could also see she could see me now too, because she had stopped her pounding and was smiling and waving at me through the glass. I was annoyed, but not at Marjorie, she was all right and looked to be in some sort of trouble, it was the thought that was trying to break through the fog in my brain, a vague impression I was standing there only in my underwear, though I was still too groggy to stop myself from swinging the door wide.

"Oh, Chris. Thank God I caught you before you left for work. You have to come right away!"

Marjorie was looking at me with a mixture of anxiety and embarrassment.

"Wha—" My tongue wasn't connected up properly yet. "What time is it?"

"Ten to six," she said. "I'm so sorry for waking you so early, but you have to come. You have to come right away, I can't stand it!"

"Wha—" I repeated. Yeah, I was a real brain surgeon this morning, but if she was right about the time being ten to six, I had only been asleep for two hours — yesterday had been a long day and night at the winery — and I needed a full eight and a half hours or the rest of the day I'm just damaged goods.

She laughed suddenly, still embarrassed at me standing there and turned me around by the shoulder. "Go get some pants on and come to the house. I'll pour you some coffee. But, hurry!"

I lived in the granny flat behind Marjorie's house so I didn't have far to go, just along the pea-gravel path through her extensive garden past the persimmon and pear trees to her back porch. I had pants and a shirt on now, and had decided what the heck and put on shoes and socks as well.

2

The pea-gravel tended to be sharp and I have sensitive feet. She was there waiting for me with the door wide, thrusting a mug of steaming coffee into my hands. Her anxiety was overcoming her embarrassment or maybe she was just relieved I had come fully dressed.

"What's the trouble?"

"Thank God you're here, Chris. I just didn't know what to do, and I was so worried you had already left for work."

"Yeah, you said that before." My brain was coming alive as I sipped at the coffee. "What's the problem?"

"I need you to catch a lizard."

"A lizard?" I tried to keep the incredulity out of my voice.

"Yes, I was washing up in the kitchen this morning and it scared me half to death! There by the sink." She was still keeping her distance.

"I don't see it." I was looking all around.

"No, you don't understand. I've already caught it. It's there, under the bar stools, beneath the plastic bowl."

I saw the plastic container overturned on the floor. It was sort of see-through, and I could just make out something long and slender captured underneath it.

"Could you catch it and put it outside?" Marjorie asked quaking with revulsion. "The thought of touching it just gives me the shivers."

It was my turn to laugh. "Okay, hold my coffee." She did, and I got down on the floor and shouldered aside the bar-stools and got into position. It was a matter of getting my hand under the container without letting the lizard loose. That,

3

I was convinced, would surely damage our landlady-tenant relationship. I got a grip on the plastic bowl and slowly lifted it just enough to slide my hand under, and like lightning I pounced and had it in my hand.

Marjorie whooped, "You did it!" and was clapping and rejoicing as I drew it forth and peeked at the lizard now in the palm of my hand.

It was a pencil.

———

I was still groggy and knew I would most likely be out of sorts the rest of the day as I drove to work. I had taken a long shower and had had four cups of coffee, and was on my fifth even now as I tooled along in my pickup down Highway 29, but it still hadn't done any good. I had the windows down, both of them, and the wind coming in was whipping my hair something fierce and had a bitter snap to it that was keeping me awake, but all I wanted was another six and a half hours hugging my pillow. As I turned into the winery through the fieldstone gateposts with the gilded letters MC for Maverick Cellars on each, I got a shock that brought me abruptly to full wakefulness. There in the employee parking lot was Vic's SUV. The man never slept. He had said he was headed home last night right after me and wouldn't be in again until noon, and here he was still at work, but that wasn't what had given me the jolt. It was the number of Napa Valley Sheriff's cars along with the Coroner's van parked here and there taking up most of the lot.

I pulled in next to Vic's vehicle, and cut the engine and

got out. At the entrance to the winery was a deputy in uniform watching me approach.

"Who're you?" he demanded as I continued forward.

"The assistant winemaker. What's going on?"

He ignored the question and thumbed me inside. Then said in a flat voice, "Somebody will wanna talk to you, so stick around."

I headed inside and almost immediately met another deputy who demanded in a similar flat voice, "What're you doing?"

"I'm Chris Garrett. I work here."

"Well, don't go anywhere."

"Yeah, I'll stick around."

"You do that." And he thumbed me farther inside.

I could see a crowd of officials spread out along the narrow concrete aisle between the fermentation vats. The vats on this side of the winery were evenly spaced on each side, sixteen in all, and reaching ten feet or so in height. They were all made of seasoned Limosin oak built in France, disassembled and then reassembled at Maverick Cellars, and each capable of holding more than five thousand gallons of fermenting must. The crowd was mostly interested in the second to last vat on the left. I headed in that direction.

"You work here?" It was another deputy, only this one I knew. It was my friend Jeff Beckwell.

"I know, I know. Don't go anywhere."

As I drew closer Jeff grabbed my arm and held me back. "You'll wanna stay back."

"What the heck's going on?"

Above us on the catwalk Sheriff Paul Coulette's voice sounded hoarse in the wet morning air. "Okay, boys. Fish him out."

His deputies grabbed hold of Victor Miranda who was floating face down in the vat of fermenting grapes. It took three of them to hoist his body clear of the thick soup of crushed fruit and position him onto a medical gurney. Red juice dripped from his stained clothing and poured from his pockets. More juice dripped in torrents down the sides of the vat and ran across the concrete tiles below. As I watched, I knew that awful sight of Victor would stay with me a long time — his tongue swollen up, his facial muscles stiff and contorted from rigor mortis, his skin and staring eyes blackened by the grape tannins.

"That Garrett?" It was the Sheriff's hoarse voice from above.

Jeff nodded. "Yeah."

"Hang on to him," he said. "We'll wanna talk."

Chapter 2

JEFF AND I had retreated to the side on standby as the experts got on with whatever they were doing, and more officials both in and out of uniform continued to arrive and join Sheriff Coulette for private pow-wows, so we waited and watched them and I tried to get air into and out of my lungs with some regularity which I was having trouble doing ever since I had seen them pull Vic out. I wasn't surprised the Sheriff was personally investigating Vic's death, even though it may seem a little out of character. Officials in his capacity were usually not so hands on with the day-to-day procedures. Being an elected official, Coulette's main job was concerned with what most elected officials were concerned with — getting re-elected. But what made this unusual was the family connection. Coulette's sister happened to be married to Vic, which made Vic his brother-in-law. So, it was personal.

The experts stayed at it awhile, and it wasn't until they were through examining Vic and were zipping him into a body bag that Coulette seemed ready for us. He motioned and said, "Beckwell, bring him," and Jeff and I started forward, but the Sheriff didn't get the chance to talk with me just yet. Vic's wife Patricia had arrived with Vic's business partner Benny Garcia in tow, and she swept into the winery like a hurricane.

"Victor!" she wailed with volume, splitting the air to the rafters. "Oh, my GAWD!" All activity in the winery came to a halt at the spectacle of Patricia as she pushed and shoved her way through to the gurney and her husband's prostrate body, and then all at once threw herself atop Vic. Of course, the gurney immediately toppled and collapsed under the weight, sending both her and Vic alarmingly to the floor. To make matters worse, as they went down, the support mechanism of the gurney caught hold of her skirt and stripped the fabric off with astonishing ease revealing more of Patricia to all of us than we ever wanted to see.

It all happened so fast that for a moment nobody moved, then everybody moved at once, and I happened to get to her just as Coulette did, me with one of her arms and him with the other. It wasn't that I was faster off the mark, I just happened to be closer. Jeff, who happened to be furthest from her, did the sensible thing and went for her skirt instead. Patricia was still wailing, though it was coming out now much too dry to carry far, and was still on top of Vic who had also slipped out of his body bag with his swollen tongue and his tannin-stained eyes staring out at nothing.

What brought her wailing around though was not her brother or my rescue, or seeing her dead husband's face, but the sound of ripping skirt. It was better than a bucket of cold water. In his haste, Jeff, to his chagrin, had pulled instead of coaxed and most of her garment had remained attached to the gurney. I happened to recognize the label, and it hadn't come off the rack.

"What're you doing, you imbecile!" Patricia screeched. Sheriff Coulette and I got her to her feet, but she shoved us away and righted herself, taking what was left of the mangled skirt from Jeff.

"I'm so sorry," Jeff said, lamely. "The material looked tougher than that!"

"You oaf!" Patricia attempted to cover herself with the torn clothes. The Sheriff tried to help her, but she was having none of that, yelling through tears, "Don't touch me!" and marched unaided toward the winery office.

Benny had finally caught up to the commotion and was watching her storm off along with everybody else. He was pale and out of breath, but who wouldn't be chauffeuring Patricia around under normal circumstances, much less on a day like this.

"The Napa Valley Opera," Benny said taking in breath, "has nothing on her." He started after her. "I'll see if she needs a glass of water or something."

The Sheriff just looked pained, but whether the pain

was on account of his sister's plight or for how she made him feel especially in his ass region I couldn't tell. He turned the pained look toward his deputy.

Jeff was apologetic. "I'm sorry, sir. I realize, that was a fashion don't."

The Sheriff waved a hand. "Skip it," he said and took in a big load of air, clear down to his middle and let it out. I guess there just wasn't enough air in the building. "You and Garrett, friends?"

"Since Junior High," Jeff said and winked at me.

Coulette nodded and looked in my direction. I realized he was sizing me up, so I thought I might as well do the same. Having heard somebody once refer to politics as Hollywood for unattractive people, I thought the Sheriff fit his role perfectly. He was certainly not handsome, all his features were too big for his face for that description, but he would've made a great character actor if the role called for say a four star general or something. He was probably in his mid-fifties, and his shirt collar was too tight, which made his neck look thick, and he was scowling at me, which didn't help his looks any. "When did you last see Vic?"

"Late," I said. "A little before three."

"You know how this happened?"

"No. I was hoping you'd tell me."

The Sheriff's scowl became more pronounced. "It's forensics' best guess this happened between three and four this morning."

"Who found him?"

"Your cellar master." He glanced at his deputy. "Got his name?"

"Yeah, and it's a mouthful," Jeff said grinning and quickly pulled out his notepad and read, "Álvaro Alonzo Vladimir Peron Padilla Rodriguez Jimenez."

The Sheriff looked skeptical though I don't know why, Jeff had it down correctly. "Vladimir?"

"I had him spell it out," Jeff said. "Maybe he's one of them Russian-Mexicans."

"It could happen," I added helpfully.

"I can do without the comedy," the Sheriff snapped. "Okay, Garrett, let's hear it."

So I filled him in. The Sheriff wasn't my only audience, many of the officials crowding the winery wanted to get my version of things, and Coulette let me go on without a lot of questions, maybe because what was happening work wise around Maverick Cellars wasn't that unusual. I took them over the last few weeks, touching on all the craziness that sets in during fall crush, the threat of rain earlier in the week that had pushed up our harvesting schedule, especially the last couple of days when not only grapes were feeling squeezed, everybody at Maverick Cellars was too, caught under the brutal workload as fruit kept stacking up everywhere and with all our tank space already loaded to capacity. Nobody was getting much sleep, Vic included. The only thing we could do was keep picking, so we did and tried to find someplace to put it all. It wasn't until late yesterday that we finally got on top of things and work slowed down somewhat. Vic had decided to let the troops go home and get some sleep, and everybody did, like war-weary survivors.

As I told my story, Patricia had come out of the office to listen, supported again on Benny's arm, her skirt now back in place and pinned together nicely. Everybody regarded her as she approached, but from the looks of her, no more theatrics were in store. She was dabbing with a tissue at her eyes. "Don't mind me," she said with a shy smile. "I'm all right, now. I just want to hear."

Coulette turned back to me.

"Go on."

"Well," I said. "Vic needed the anthocyanin numbers checked. That job didn't take both of us, so he told me to go home and get some rest; he'd take care of it. I went. I was spent. Neither of us had had more than a few hours sleep in a week. He told me he was headed home himself—"

Coulette held me up a moment and got the attention of the Medical Examiner. "Danielle, just a minute."

The M.E. was with two paramedics in the process of wheeling Vic, who was now back in his body bag and properly positioned on the gurney, to the awaiting ambulance.

Patricia, her eyes very large, didn't make any moves to pounce, though the way the paramedics were watching her, you'd have thought they expected her to.

The M.E. stepped aside to let the medics and gurney roll by and removed her medical smock.

"Got a cause of death?" Coulette asked.

"Well, Paul," she said joining us, "I won't say officially until we're finished with our examination. Unofficially, I'd say it was an accident."

"An accident!" Patricia gasped.

Benny still holding her arm soothed with gentle pats. "That's right," he said. "What did I tell you?"

The Sheriff gave a quick eye toward them, but saw his sister wasn't set to erupt so went on to the M.E, "You think he just slipped and fell in—"

"—And drowned, yes I do. His lungs are full of fluid. No physical marks on the body besides the obvious grape juice staining. With active fermentations of this size, there's plenty of carbon dioxide around to cause asphyxiation."

Everybody was nodding, Patricia and Benny, many of the other officials standing around, even the Sheriff. It was the plausible explanation, and what everybody was obviously thinking had happened, I could see that, but I wanted to object. And I would have if I hadn't felt Jeff's hand on my shoulder. A quick glance from him said plainly 'Now's not the time.' So, I bit my lip, but anybody working around fermenting wine knew about the potential hazards. One quick way to drive the point home with new employees was to dangle them over an active tank, in a kind of initiation rite and let them get a lung full of the gases coming off. Nobody needed to go through that lesson a second time. Snot, tears and everything else your body could expel would shoot forth from every orifice. It was a crude yet powerful reminder not to take the danger for granted, and people usually didn't. How the M.E. was describing things seemed ridiculous to me, especially in

Vic's case with all his experience, more than almost anybody in the whole Valley. The winery was well ventilated, and if prolonged exposure to CO_2 was unavoidable, we had oxygen masks. Double-checking the anthocyanins, the color components extracted from grape skins during fermentation, didn't take long anyway. Getting a juice sample took seconds and posed hardly any risk. It would have been a silly and stupid accident, and Vic had been neither silly nor stupid.

The M.E. must have noticed my difficulty with her theory because she was quick to caveat. "Again, we won't know for sure until the lab work is done. It could easily have been a heart attack. Not uncommon for someone his age."

I watched the Sheriff mull this over as he let her leave. He absently returned to the fermentation vat for another look, and Jeff and I tagged along, I guess because we expected him to make some sort of pronouncement. So did everybody else, but he didn't say anything, just continued to mull. We followed him up the stairs to the catwalk. A deputy at the vat was trying without success to snag a set of eyeglasses still floating in the must. He was batting at them with his police baton. The eyeglasses remained stubbornly out of reach.

Coulette watched this for a second before glancing at me. "Those look like Vic's to you?"

They did, so I said, "Yeah," then because it was puzzling, I added, "but I don't get it."

"What don't you get?" The Sheriff was still watching his deputy.

"Well, Vic usually left his glasses on this shelf." I pointed at the shelf only a few steps away. It was actually a steel beam that structurally supported part of the catwalk that circled the vats.

Coulette glanced at the shelf, then at me. "So, what's your point?" I could tell his patience was wearing thin.

"My point is — I can't understand why they're in the must."

"Understand? Seems clear enough. Vic fell in and his glasses went in with him." Off to his left, Jeff was warning me again with his eyes to lay off, but I felt myself pressing on anyway.

"It's just not how he worked," I said. "We're checking musts all the time, taking the brix, monitoring fermentation rates, punching down the cap, checking color extraction, tasting — Vic never used his glasses for that kind of work. They were always falling out of his pocket into the must. Swinging in the way on those chains around his neck. That's why he always put them on the shelf. It was a habit with him. Ask anybody."

I waited for a reaction, but Coulette didn't make one. Jeff had decided his eyes weren't communicating very well and was giving them a good rubbing. I looked down and most of the people below us were still listening, Patricia and Benny included.

I went on stubbornly.

"If it was a heart attack, all right. He clutches his chest, loses his balance and topples in, sucks up a lung full of juice, end of story. But if he was working like the Medical Examiner said, was getting a sample and because he was careless, asphyxiated on CO_2, why aren't his glasses on that shelf?"

The Sheriff harrumphed. Jeff remained quiet, thinking it over. Many of the officials below shook their heads, not buying it. Patricia and Benny were listening intently to what I was saying.

"I can't believe," I said, "that Vic, who had worked around wine for over thirty-five years, with that kind of experience, would have such a silly, preventable accident. He was well aware of the risks. He could've written a book on it — ten books. It doesn't make any sense."

It was then that something happened that sealed it in the Sheriff's opinion, along with everybody else who was watching. Jeff caught sight of it first. His fellow deputy still fishing for Vic's glasses with his baton slipped suddenly over the lip of the oak vat, his feet heading into the air, having succumbed to the very risk I was pressing them as obviously impossible for Vic. The alarm went up at once from nearly everybody on hand, and reacting quickly, Jeff grabbed the deputy's feet before he went in completely and levered him out, though not before the deputy's arms and a good part of his head and chest had taken a liberal dunk in the crushed grapes.

Safely out of the vat, the deputy's eyes rolled and fluttered. Grape muck was in his hair and dripped down his face. A throat full of juice welled up, and he hunched over vigorously hacking. He had gotten too close and tried to breathe an unbreathable gas. And failed.

When Jeff and the Sheriff got him steady again on his feet, breathing oxygen this time, both turned as if on cue and gave me the same look. You didn't have to be a mind reader to guess what both were thinking. Smooth move, Sherlock. Case closed.

Chapter 3

"I SAW HIS foot sticking out of the grapes," Álvaro said reliving the event. "Well, actually just his shoe."

"His shoe?" I prompted to get him past that particular pothole. Álvaro was looking a little green to me.

He nodded and swallowed a couple times. "I thought, who would throw a shoe in the wine? Crazy, huh?"

I nodded back.

It was well past noon before the last of Coulette's people finished with their investigation and departed. The Tasting Room had been closed down for the remainder of the day, which was sensible considering the state of mind everybody in the winery was currently suffering under, not to mention the public relations debacle of having your winemaker die on the premises and the unwanted attention that kind of thing attracted. Benny thought it prudent to lock the gate and put out the *closed* sign, especially when the steady drumbeat of news hounds hammering at the door and the phone had pushed the women in the front office nearly over the edge. He had also wanted to send everybody home for the duration if it was possible, but there was way too much to do around the place. Like what we were doing just then, emptying the vat of wine Vic had drowned in.

Nobody paid me much mind after the deputy had taken his plunge. As far as my opinion went, I was written off, but I still didn't buy the idea that Vic's death was his own damn fault, no matter what everybody else thought. Ever since I saw them pull him from that vat, my feelings had been jumbled; sadness and grief certainly, but what I felt most I was beginning to realize was anger. It made me angry to think that anybody who knew Vic at all would believe he could be so careless, but stalking around the place kicking buckets and snarling wouldn't help the work get done any faster, and besides, Jeff had told me before he left with the rest of the officials that he would get us an update on Vic's Cause Of Death as soon as it was available. It might've been a heart attack after all.

So I was keeping the lid on as I wheeled a must pump up to where we were going to use it to flush out the tank. I asked Álvaro off hand, "What made you look in the vat?"

Álvaro pointed above. "The lid was open. I thought somebody had forgotten, so I went to shut it."

"And then you saw the shoe," said our intern Henri Etiene,

his French accent pronounced, being with us only since the beginning of summer. He was assisting Álvaro and me in attaching a large hose to the nozzle on the side of the vat.

"Yeah, I saw it," said Álvaro.

"And then you saw Vic was still wearing the shoe," Henri added.

Álvaro gulped. "That is when I called 911."

Benny, having driven Patricia home and then returned was now supervising the winemaking activities in Vic's absence. Not that there was a lot to supervise. Everybody knew what their job was and how to do it, and Vic and I had spent a great deal of time before crush discussing what he wanted done and as far as I knew we were still following that plan. Of course, Benny's plan might just be finding a moment's peace from the incessant phone calls in the front office and had ducked out.

"Chris." Benny waved me over. So I joined him a few steps to the side. He was winding up to something I could tell. "Vic always thought very highly of you, and since he's not around," he grabbed my arm and gave it a squeeze and I watched him swallow a couple of times before he could go on, "you'll have to shoulder a lot of the burden around here for the time being. Keep this machine rolling along, huh?" He tried to smile.

I nodded. "Sure."

"Think you can handle things?"

"No problem. We'll get it done," I said and hoped I sounded confident. "Don't worry."

He gave me a measured stare and seemed satisfied.

"Good," he said.

Obaldo "Benny" Garcia and Victor Miranda had started Maverick Cellars together in the sixties back when Napa was better known for its mental hospital than for its premium wine. They had begun with ten acres of head-pruned Zinfandel planted sometime before Prohibition and over the next forty years had turned it and a dream into a $50 million business. Victor had made the wines and Benny had sold them and together with a tremendous amount of guts and hard work they had made Maverick Cellars a household name. But now there was only one of them to carry on, and I realized suddenly Benny wasn't just asking me to take on a bigger job, he was asking me to replace Vic.

He gave my arm another squeeze, and we both turned back to the job at hand.

Álvaro and Henri were ready with the hose so we set about flushing the soiled must from the fermentation vat — all five thousand gallons of it — and with that kind of volume it would take a few minutes. The hose was transparent so once it began the fermenting mess could be seen flowing down its length. The hose snaked its way out through the winery doors to a portable tank fixed to the back of a flatbed truck outside just beyond the crush pad. Later, the truck would haul away the soiled must for composting.

"Such a waste, throwing it out," Henri pronounced, as the pomace bucked and surged its way past him through the hose. "What, a half million dollars in juice?"

I saw Benny wince at the number. Henri was right. I could

see where he was coming from. The replacement value of the fruit alone that insurance would likely cover was nothing near the potential value of the finished wine, which in all honesty was way upwards of that.

"It was just like Vic to end his life in a vat of our finest wine," Benny's gravelly voice rumbled. "With him, it was always the best and nothing but the best." I could see Henri and Álvaro smiling back at him as I was trying to do, but it felt awkward. Benny's attempt at levity didn't entirely take the sting out, even for him. That kind of monetary hit would be a heavy blow for any business.

"Why not save it, you know just filter it?" Henri went on. He hadn't put two and two together just yet.

"It is like finding a finger in your fries at the drive-thru." Álvaro offered patiently. "Not good for business."

"Oh, that had not occurred to me," Henri said, clarity finally sinking in. Indelicate as Álvaro had been, the vulgar truth of the matter was Maverick Cellars could ill afford to have its image tarnished by the idea of a dead winemaker macerating in his own wine.

I caught a glimpse of Jeff returning through the doorway outside, still in his deputy uniform following our pomace hose back along its length and I thought, hopefully, bringing word about the official line on Vic's death. He had caught the last of what Álvaro had said, and added, "Should've seen what we found in the County Hospital's cafeteria a while back."

I saw how Benny was taking that and quickly made the kill it motion with my hand hacking at my throat and luckily

Jeff caught sight of that too.

Glancing at the vat, he finished, lamely, "Yeah, wouldn't be very quaffable."

Benny turned toward the offices. "Well, I'll leave it up to you," his voice sounding more gravelly than ever, and as he ambled off, I heard him murmur to no one in particular, "This is the worst thing that has ever happened."

Jeff waited until I looked back at him to ask, "Got a minute?"

I said, "Yeah, c'mon," and led him outside across the crush pad toward the flatbed. I needed to make sure the hose wasn't plugging up.

"It's official," he said as we went. "Vic drowned. Death caused by juice and wine pomace sucked into the lungs, probably after inadvertent CO_2 asphyxiation."

I stopped next to the flatbed and saw that the wine and pomace was flowing out the end of the hose just fine.

Jeff continued, "Your boss didn't have a heart attack. It was just an accident, plain and simple. Anyway, that's what the Sheriff's writing up. It's a done deal."

I didn't say anything, probably because hearing that the accident was now official had caught me off balance. I knew from the way everybody had been acting up until then — the Sheriff, the other officials, even Patricia and Benny — this would end up being the official line, but I guess I just didn't want to hear it.

Jeff knew my look better than almost anybody and could see I wasn't accepting the official line. "I don't know what else to tell you."

"What about the glasses?"

"That again?" It was clear what he thought about my earlier observation. I knew his face nearly as well as he knew mine. "Maybe, this one time he forgot and had them on." But as Jeff was saying it, I also knew that he wasn't buying it either. "I knew this was gonna piss you off."

"Of course, I'm pissed. I'm pissed Vic's dead. But I'm more pissed that everybody thinks he killed himself."

"Accidentally."

"That's right, accidentally. It was his own damn fault. He was a dope and he was careless and he accidentally killed himself. That's the official line."

"Yep, and you're pissed about it."

"It makes me so damn pissed I feel like I'm gonna choke."

Jeff nodded. "I can see that."

"You knew Vic. Was he a dope?"

"I knew Vic. He was certainly not a dope."

"You know me. Am I a dope?"

"You are definitely not a dope."

"And you're not a dope."

"The jury's still out on that. I may be a dope."

I was still mad, but I had to smile a little. "Trust me, you're not a dope."

"Okay, I'm not a dope."

"And I'm not a dope, and Vic was not a dope, and only a dope would die like that. So where does that leave us?"

"I hate it when you do this. It means the accident was probably not an accident."

"And if it wasn't an accident, those who think it was are probably—"

"Dopes."

"Yep."

Jeff thought about it a moment. "Kind of pisses me off too."

Chapter 4

JEFF DIDN'T STICK around. He had been on nightshift when the call came in this morning about Vic and when he left Maverick Cellars had headed home to get some shuteye before he had to be on the job again this evening. I stifled a yawn, the one hundred and fortieth I had stifled so far today, and tried not to think about when I'd get a chance again to shut my eyes.

Anthony Picozzi, Maverick Cellars' vineyard manager, had called me on his cell soon after Jeff had left and said we needed to talk. He hadn't elaborated, but I figured I already knew what he wanted to talk about and it wasn't about Vic. More than likely, he wanted to go over the harvesting schedule again. I told him I'd meet up with him as soon as

I could get away. Tony was currently at our new holdings high on Spring Mountain, mostly Cabernet Sauvignon and some Cabernet Franc, that Maverick Cellars had acquired a few years ago, mountain fruit that was showing promise. I also told him I wanted another look at the fruit before he got the picking crews rolling.

I needed tank space, more than just the vat Vic had fallen into, emptied and sanitized before we could bring in any more of Tony's fruit, so I started Álvaro and Henri barreling down tank six and tank seven, the pressed wine in them having finished primary. Seeing that they had everything in hand, I got rolling and it wasn't long before I was traveling up Spring Mountain Road heading west out of St. Helena.

The fruit wasn't the only thing on my mind. I was thinking about what Jeff and I had talked about. Foremost was the thought that if I was sticking to the notion that Vic hadn't just slipped and fell into that vat and drowned, but more likely was pushed, who did the pushing? The more I asked myself that question, the more I drew a blank. Vic certainly could be difficult at times, and even an outright tyrant, but enough of a thorn in somebody's side for somebody to kill him? I just didn't know. I had met or knew most of his relatives and friends and could guess at some of his enemies, but did any of them stand out in my mind as his murderer? The more I tried to get my mind around it the more of a headache I got.

I was driving my '66 Chevy pickup, sky blue with white side-panels that used to be my Dad's. You don't see many 66's on the road these days, especially in good condition, and though it was now technically mine, I still thought of it as his and tried my best to baby it like he used to do.

I shifted into lower gear and sailed through another tight turn. The twisting road I was on switched back and forth sometimes sharply as it snaked its way out of the Valley, cutting severely into the side of the mountain or swinging out over a deep gorge made by the roaring creek below. Eventually, the road would weave all the way up and over the Mayacamas Mountains and down the other side into Sonoma County.

A few miles further up the mountain I turned off the road and rambled into the hills on a twisting byway that soon left its own narrow stretch of pavement behind. Continuing along this gravel spur for another mile or so, I finally reached our vineyard holdings.

Tony's green quad-runner was parked next to the fence, with a yellow polypropylene spray tank attached to the rack on its back. I pulled my pickup off the road on this side of the fence, stepped on the parking brake and killed the engine. Tony was striding down a row of vines toward me, his face brightening.

"Hey, paisano!" he bellowed as he got to me and reached over the fence to crush my hand.

"Hey, Tony," I said, trying unsuccessfully to extricate myself from his handshake.

Anthony Picozzi had been with Vic and Benny almost from the start, and as far as I knew had spent most of that time in the vineyard. The wrinkles around his eyes were now deep furrows from long hours squinting in the sun. What you remembered most about him, though, were his callused hands, especially after experiencing one of his bone-crushing greetings.

I shook blood back into my fingers. "So you think the fruit's ready?"

Tony winked at me. "C'mon," he said, "I'll show you." And waited for me to follow him into the vineyard.

I grabbed a plastic bag and my refractometer from the truck and hopped the fence. Soon both of us were sampling berries as we tread the trellised rows. I also took individual grapes from clusters here and there amongst the rows and dropped them into my plastic bag. Once I had a good sample, I could squeeze the berries to release their juices and get an overall view of how the vineyard's sugar levels were progressing.

"Look at the clusters," Tony said proudly, caressing them gently. "So heavy, like a Brahma bull."

I nodded and had to smile. The fruit did look good.

"And sweet," Tony went on. "They taste great! I think they're ready."

I thought he might be right. The clusters were a deep purple black, and the grapes were very sweet — their skins soft to the touch, not hard and tight like unripe fruit. I liked the taste, and chewed the skins a little and liked the feel of the tannins. But some of the seeds still had a tinge of green to them, and didn't crunch the way I liked when chewed.

"I know Vic wanted to wait." Tony was looking earnestly at me. "But the fruit looks ready now. And since the unfortunate accident, we have tank space for it earlier than we thought we would. I don't see why we should wait."

This was what Tony had called me about.

"But Tony," I said, "you would've picked the fruit a week ago."

"Yeah, so what's your point?"

"My point is I think we'll wait a couple more days."

Tony eyed me for a long moment through his wrinkled brows and then spat, "You're just like Vic!"

We continued to sample as we walked, but to be honest, what was most on my mind was not the ripeness of the fruit. "Hey, Tony?" I asked. "How long did you know Vic?"

Tony gave me a far away glance. "I knew Vic over thirty-five years."

We kept moving along the terraced hillside.

"You know of anybody who may have had it in for him?"

Tony stopped abruptly. "Heard you're having trouble with it being an accident."

I stopped next to him. "So you buy it? The accident, I mean?"

"Sure, why not? It's awful." He picked a leaf off a nearby shoot and absently inspected it. "But it's happened before."

"But to Vic?"

Tony shrugged. "It could happen to anybody."

I nodded, but I still wasn't convinced.

"Vic could be a pain in the ass, but enough for somebody to kill him?" He answered his own question. "I don't think so."

Knowing Tony like I did, I wasn't going to get anything more out of him. Whatever he knew, if he knew anything at all, he wasn't sharing it with me.

Tony threw his arm over my neck good-naturedly and gave my shoulder a squeeze, damn near Vulcan neck-pinching me. He motioned at my bag of grapes, "C'mon. Tell me the verdict."

I finished kneading the berries and put some of the juice on the glass of the refractometer. I then looked through the prism and took a Brix reading. Tony watched me expectantly.

"They're ready, huh? Like I said?"

I looked at him. "Yep, in a couple days."

I sympathized with Tony, to a degree, as I headed back down the mountain. Part of the reason Maverick Cellars was having tank space limitations, and Tony was pushing so hard to pick, was on account of this new vineyard expansion taken on by Vic and Benny a few years back with the help of tech-wizard, Gerry Zacks. Zacks had recently swept into the Valley having procured an overwhelming passion for wine along with $92 million in venture capital and wouldn't be satisfied until he owned his own piece of the good life. He'd put up most of the money to purchase the land and for that was rewarded partnership in one of Napa's premiere labels. Maverick Cellars' holdings had increased overnight, with one hundred fifty eight acres of prime Napa Valley fruit on Spring Mountain, much of it on newly planted scions just now beginning to bear.

It was going to be tight right up to the end whether or not we would get all the fruit processed in time. I had acted confidently in front of Tony, but to be honest, I didn't want to dwell too much on it, especially now that all the key decisions and their repercussions rested solely on my shoulders. I might start feeling overwhelmed and begin to panic, and with all the switchbacks and steep turns I had to navigate as I headed down Spring Mountain Road I might drive right off the edge and have an accident of my own. But I did all right.

The panic nearly had me though when I finally got back to the winery. I thought I had left everything in good hands, Álvaro was a rock and knew his job and would keep everybody moving, and had expected things to have progressed nicely, so when I stepped foot inside I wasn't prepared for all the commotion going on. Barrels that had been brought down to the floor to be filled and then restacked were being restacked empty, and the fermentation tanks as far as I could see were still completely full. Nobody was moving forward with the tasks I had initially set out. I had barely taken all this in when Álvaro rolled up next to me on the forklift.

"Eric is here," he said, as if that explained everything, which of course it did.

Eric Miranda was Vic's son and like what often happens with sons and fathers, they hadn't exactly seen eye to eye. Against Vic's wishes, Eric had shown little interest if not outright disdain in the day-to-day dealings of the winery and had actively stayed away from the family business. What he had stayed away doing, I could only guess at, but I think there had been a restaurant he was financially involved in at one time and I knew he did a lot of traveling but for what reason beyond recreation I hadn't heard. I only knew it had nothing to do with Maverick Cellars. As far as it goes, he had set foot inside the winery twice in the past year, once to drink through the reserve wines with a bunch of his buddies and the second time to abscond with six cases of aged beauties kept under lock and key in the wine library. That had been the peak of his interest in Maverick Cellars or so it had seemed, until now.

"Chris, what the hell!" Eric yelled from across the hundred or so barrels still crowding the floor space between us. He started zigzagging through them toward me, his voice still elevated. "Everybody says this was your idiotic idea!"

I waited until he cleared the barrels and got to me. "What's the problem, Eric?"

"The problem? Just look at this mess! Don't you know the schedule around here? We've got the barrel tasting dinner! We should be setting up for that, and what do you do? You go and tear down all the stacks!"

The barrel tasting dinner — twice a year, a select group of Maverick Cellars patrons were invited to dine amongst the barrels and taste the current releases along with some of the wines still maturing in wood. It was a very popular event and I was of course aware of it and knew it was scheduled for tomorrow night, but with what had happened to Vic I had assumed it would be postponed or cancelled or something — and for the moment Eric's onslaught had me off balance. I managed to say, "That's tomorrow, if we're still going through with it."

"Of course we're going through with it!" he snapped. "We

got people flying in from all over the country! From Atlanta, and Florida, even New York! We're not gonna just cancel it!"

I realized at once I needed to go on the offensive or Eric would continue steamrolling me. "There's no reason to panic."

"I'm not panicking."

"That's good, because there's no reason to. If we're going through with the dinner like you say—"

"—We *are* going through with it!"

"Okay. Then if we're going through with it, what I'm saying is there's plenty of time to empty these vats and fill these barrels and still have everything ready by tomorrow."

"We're not postponing the dinner!"

"I realize that. Don't worry. We've got plenty of time, believe me, and besides, the real charm of holding the dinner here in the first place is that everybody knows this is the real deal, a working winery. So why don't we let these people get on with their work."

"Yeah, well, as much as you might prefer it, this business isn't just winemaking, it's wine selling!" With that parting shot he wheeled and headed out. I always hate it when people think they've won an argument just by being the first to leave.

I glanced around and noticed Álvaro and the rest of the crew still watching me.

"Nice having him clear that up," I said.

I got some chuckles from the crew.

From his forklift, Álvaro said, "What now, jefe?"

"We've got barrels to fill," I said. "Let's hop to it."

Chapter 5

I'D LIKE TO say that we got both tanks emptied and all the barrels filled with plenty of time to spare, just to thumb Eric a good one in the eye on account of his earlier antics, but we didn't. There just weren't enough hours in the day. Having Vic's son land in the middle of my scheduling and start ordering people about didn't help matters either, so we managed to empty and clean only one of the tanks and fill only half the barrels before I finally had to call it quits. Everybody looked dead on their feet, and if they were only half as tired as I felt, Maverick Cellars was asking too much from them. Besides, when people get too tired accidents can happen, and we had had one too many accidents already today. I told them to leave the barrels down and head home. We would pick up where we left off tomorrow. That had been around eight-thirty.

So I headed home myself.

The light at the end of the day as I drove into the drive-way was about the same hue as it had been when I had left this morning. I pushed on the brake and killed the engine and sat there for a bit to collect myself. I was thinking that I hadn't had anything to eat all day, and should probably put my mind on that, but my head hurt, probably because I hadn't eaten anything all day, along with the rest of my aching body, and I had all but decided that sleep would be the most deli-cious dish I could probably manage right now, maybe if I just stretched out along the seat right here, when I was startled again with banging on my side window. Standing next to the window was Marjorie.

"Are you alright?" I heard her say though the glass. "You were just sitting out here, staring, and I—"

I opened the truck door, and she backed up a step.

"Oh, honey," she said, "you look all caved in."

"That's the way I feel. It's been—" And I shut the door, nearly clipping my fingers in it.

"Watch out!" she winced.

I shook my fingers and rubbed at them. "It's been—" I trailed off. Been what? Where did my brain go? I was losing my train of thought. I just stood there trying to think, rub-bing my clipped fingers.

"I heard about what happened to your Vic. On the T.V."

I nodded.

"Have you had any supper?"

"I was thinking of just going to bed. I think I'm too tired to eat."

"Nonsense. You come inside with me." She took me by the arm and led me toward her back porch and just then I caught a whiff of something wonderful emanating from the kitchen. It gave me a new thought, which was grand, maybe before resting my aching head and body in slumber for the rest of the decade, which was about how long I felt I was behind on my sleep now anyway, it wouldn't hurt to have a little bite to eat.

So I was soon seated on one of the barstools at the counter in Marjorie's kitchen, the same barstools I had shouldered aside to catch the lizard this morning, watching her fiddle with preparations on the stove.

"What's on the menu?"

"Hope you like beef stew."

It couldn't have been more perfect. "With vegetables from the garden?"

"Of course." She was ladling out a healthy portion in a big bowl, and I had already noticed the baguette on the cutting board for dipping.

Now that I had committed to the idea of eating I was hungry enough to eat my hand, but this morning's lizard event was still present in my mind and I had a confession to make. I hadn't actually shown her what I had caught was only a pencil. She wouldn't look at it at the time, nor could I say anything about it because she wouldn't let me and had chased me out so I wouldn't be late to work. But I had to let her know sooner or later, because it meant the lizard was probably still loose in the house.

"Thank you again for catching that lizard. It's the cat that brings them in."

"Listen, Marjorie, about the lizard—"

She set the stew before me on the counter. "No talking, just eat." And she was back at the cutting board, chopping the baguette down to size. Perhaps telling her later about the pencil was best, so I hoisted up a spoon and did as she ordered. Who was I to argue? I had four bowls.

———

The next day started bright and early. I had slept straight through the night almost nine hours without any interruptions by landladies, or for that matter, landmines, not that a landmine would've woken me up anyway if, for instance, one had happened to have gone off outside my window. Once back at Maverick Cellars we got at the tanks and barrels and before too long had everything finished up with plenty of time to spare. It's amazing what a full night of sleep can do, not only for me, but also for the entire cellar crew. I wouldn't say that there was a extra spring in everybody's step — the loss of Vic was still too palpable — but the work was completed quickly and efficiently, and when the caterers arrived and began setting up for the Barrel Tasting Dinner, they were none the wiser that the floor space had been covered only forty-five minutes earlier from one end to the other with hoses and equipment and barrels and forklifts and scurrying cellar rats — the two legged kind — and completely inaccessible. The disappointing part was that Eric never turned up even once during the whole day for his eye thumbing.

The food preparations were being carried out in the winery kitchen by the caterer's competent staff, who had also taken care of a great deal of the winery's party decorations, the most prominent of which was a string of lights strung above the concourse between the barrel stacks where the tables were set and the patrons would be dining, with umbrellas in two different colors, tomato and mustard — I had been corrected earlier when inadvertently referring to them as red and yellow — clustered beneath them acting as lampshades. I had to admit the effect was dramatic, softening the more industrial aspects of the winery and setting off and warming the stacks of barrels on both sides, making the place feel very festive. Now if we could only carry off the event in a festive manner.

I personally wasn't feeling very festive. The loss of Vic was too present in everything that was going on, and I could see my feelings about the matter reflected in everybody else who had to come to me now instead of him for some decision or order that needed to be made. I had decided the best thing to do was to treat the whole thing as Vic's wake, and smile encouragingly and act buoyantly when the occasion demanded or more solemnly when that was more appropriate. But mostly I just tried to keep the crew focused on the job at hand, and so far that was working.

About half of the invited guests had already arrived and others were joining them every moment. Jeff in a jacket and tie and my personal guest was helping me set up bottles and glasses at the wine-pouring table.

"Why am I here again?" he asked, tugging uncomfortably at his shirt collar. The knot of his tie was loose and his collar didn't look too tight, but his face was red and he was still having trouble getting the proper amount of oxygen.

"You're here to help me."

"Not to pour wine?"

"No. You're here because everybody who knew Vic or had any dealings with him will most likely be here. And we both figured—"

"Both of us?"

"Yes. We both figured it would be a good idea to at least get a look at them."

"Even if we don't know who we're looking at."

"We'll know who we're looking at, we just won't know if they did it or not."

"Oh, yeah." Jeff straightened his shoulders and took in a big breath, and glanced around. His coat sleeves were riding up on him, even though I knew the cut of the jacket was just fine. "I knew there was a catch."

Jeff also knew better than most that once Cause Of Death is officially established, like Vic's drowning being accepted as accidental, it takes more than just a suspicion of foul play to reopen the investigation. It takes strong, credible evidence to the contrary, and if we ever hoped the Sheriff's Department would reopen the investigation of Vic's death, it was Jeff and I who more than likely had to find them some evidence. He was just being difficult because I made him wear a tie and jacket.

Some patrons approached us, an elderly man and woman — the Vancourtlands — and we helped them with glasses and poured them some wine, and with them it was a moment to be solemn, not gay, as they gave us their sober condolences concerning Vic. I shook their hands and they moved off without too much effort. Jeff was watching them like a hawk.

"Do I know them?"

"No. They just flew in from Chicago. He's a thoracic surgeon, retired."

"I should hope so. Did you see how his hands shook? I wouldn't want somebody like that operating on me!"

I had detected the hand tremors as well. We were off to a great start.

"If only we could detect a healthy motive by shaking hands," I said, "then we'd have something."

"Hey, remember in high school, the way we used to shake hands?" Off my puzzled look, Jeff went on, "C'mon, gimme your hand." It was in that schoolyard voice familiar to all who ever got talked into something they know they shouldn't get talked into.

"I'm not giving you my hand."

"Ah, c'mon. Shake my hand."

"No!"

"C'mon," he had his hand out. It had become a dare. What was I to do? So I shook it, and as he gripped my hand he curled his middle finger to tickle my palm.

I jerked my hand away. "Will you cut that out?"

He laughed. "That might get a reaction."

"Not the kind we're looking for."

He shrugged.

People kept arriving, and the first place they usually headed for was the wine-pouring table, and it wasn't too long before I was up to my elbows in business, so Jeff decided he'd mingle and left me to it. One of the nice things about wine is the sense of well being it brings — it's hard to drink it and remain uptight or irritable — and the wines were showing very well, right down the line. Usually there is the one wine, more often than not the reserve that quite honestly needs more time before it'll show best and should be decanted, but tonight even the reserves were knocking everybody's socks off. They were all a glowing tribute to Vic and his winemaking prowess.

The volume of voices was rising by the minute, and I was starting to loosen up a little myself as the more sober talk about Vic was being left behind. Smiles were coming more easily to people's faces and laughter was even bubbling up somewhere across the room, and, though it might be hard to believe, I was beginning to think maybe Eric was right about holding the dinner in spite of what had happened.

Then the Mirandas arrived. They were all there, Patricia at the center, like a Queen amidst her court, dressed in black, which was appropriate, but there was no reason the design had to be dowdy and it wasn't. With her was Benny being steadfast with his arm for support and behind her were her two children, Frances also in black with her husband Tom and Eric with his latest conquest. The others had chosen somber attire as well, befitting their bereavement, all except Eric's girl who was wearing red. She certainly didn't look bereaved, and though I would rather have said she looked flashy and out of place for the evening it would be a lie. That dress wasn't flashy, the red was a deep wine red and fit like it meant it, and I can't recall anybody ever looking more elegant. What was flashy was what was inside that dress.

People moved to greet them and there was much shaking hands and more condolences, but the crowd around my table mostly stayed put seeing that the entourage was moving this way and parted for them when they came to take a glass.

The first to arrive was Frances with Tom in tow, but I could see Tom getting caught up in conversations with some people, so Frances dropped him and sidled up to the table by herself.

"Hi Chris." Frances looked like she was holding up pretty well under the circumstances. We had gone to high school together, she had been a junior when I was a freshman, and she liked to claim I was the only reason she made it through Algebra. Juniors usually didn't associate with lowly freshmen, so having her treat me kindly, even if it was only for my proficiency in math, had been flattering. I've always liked her.

"Hi Frances. You ready for tonight?"

"God, no! But what am I to do? Get drunk I suppose."

She took a glass and got another for her husband who was still trapped a few steps away in conversation and passed it to him. He barely looked at it. But she was right back.

"How're you handing things?" she asked.

"I haven't got into a fist fight yet."

She smiled. "I know what you mean." She turned back to look at her Mother and Benny and Eric and his girl who had only made it about half way to the table. "I've felt like using my fists more than once today, myself."

"Well the day's not over. Maybe you'll get your chance."

"Oh, you think?" The thought seemed to perk her up. Her eyes were still on her family. "All I need is a few drinks in me for courage and watch out! Don't think I won't do it. I've got more of my mother in me than most people know." Which I knew was a lie. If anything, she was her father's daughter through and through. I'd never seen her raise her voice let alone throw a fit.

"Who's the girl?"

Frances gave me a look. "With Eric?"

"Yeah, with Eric. I'll admit, your brother knows how to pick 'em."

She gave me another look.

"Her name's Rosalynd Warder. You've heard of the Warders — from San Francisco?"

I hadn't.

"Their family's big in the charity game."

"Loaded?"

"Are you kidding? Of course, they're loaded. That's why Mother finds them so fascinating." Frances was nodding knowingly at me. "That's right. Mother set it up. She knows Rosalynd's mother and the two of them hatched this up because they thought they'd be so cute together. This is all according to Mother. Do I need to remind you, the Warders are loaded?"

"No. Eric seems to like the idea just fine."

"Do I need to remind you, the Warders—"

"—are loaded. No."

"You were always so smart. Eric, of course, is completely smitten."

"With her or with her money?"

"Both, certainly."

"So, she's a willing partner in all this intrigue?"

"Rosalynd? Hardly. As far as I can tell, she's just stringing him along. I find her kind of cold myself. Aloof. I don't think she has an emotional bone in her body."

We were interrupted by another guest, Jake Hubbell, from one of the brokerage houses in town, I forget which one, who pushed in next to Frances jostling her wine.

"Hey, Garrett, where's Gerry Zacks?" he asked in too loud a voice, not even apologizing to Frances for spilling her drink. "I thought he'd be at this shindig."

I helped Frances with a napkin and refilled her glass before answering. "I haven't seen him."

"I was expecting Zacks to be here."

Hubbell was plainly here for his own business, not to taste Maverick Cellars' latest releases, and tracking down the tech entrepreneur for him was not one of my high priorities. I wasn't sure Gerry even wanted to talk to him, quite frankly. Luckily, Benny had reached the table and decided to step in, having overheard the loudmouth. For that matter, who hadn't?

"I talked with Gerry earlier," Benny said. "He assured me he'd be here." Benny took Hubbell's hand like greeting a long time friend and as he shook it, steered him away from the table. "Zacks wouldn't miss it!"

"Good. That's good, 'cause I need to talk with him."

Benny was patting him on the back. "When he arrives, I'll make sure he does."

But Hubbell had been moved far enough back from the table for the rest of the Mirandas to sidle up.

Frances helped me get glasses of wine passed amongst them, starting with her mother. When I tried to give the girl in the red dress a glass, Eric intercepted and took the glass from me and offered it to her himself. Then he got a napkin for her, this time off the table, not out of my outstretched hand. Next I expected he'd be offering to brush her teeth for her. He certainly was smitten.

Behind Eric, I caught a glimpse of Jeff still on patrol meeting and greeting people and saw him shaking hands with an orthodontist from Santa Rosa, named Samuelson. Then I saw Samuelson jerk his hand away, and saw rather than heard him exclaim, "What the hell?" Yep, Jeff was getting reactions all right. It made me think this plan of picking a face from the crowd and the right face no less might actually work, if we had maybe a hundred years and were really, really lucky.

Another girl, this one I knew, was trying to catch my eye and finally did, waving to me over the shoulder of Frances and her husband Tom who were now both trapped in that same conversation from before. The waving girl was Jennifer Kimura and like Hubbell I could readily guess why she was here, and it wasn't to taste wine. So when she made it up to the table I gave her a glass anyway.

"Chris, you just must be devastated!"

"Hi Jennifer."

Jennifer Kimura was a Public Relations Consultant and could smell an embarrassing debacle from a mile off. I'll admit, Public Relations was currently a high priority at Maverick Cellars, or soon would be, and no doubt she was fishing for a commission, but nobody at Maverick Cellars had even discussed the idea of hiring a consultant.

She was nodding, being very serious. "I'm so sorry for you, and the Mirandas of course. I tried getting you on the phone when I heard what happened."

"Yeah, I'm sorry I didn't get back to you. My voice mail's been really smokin'."

"Oh, I *know*." She really emphasized the 'know'. "I *know*."

"You understand things around here have been a little hectic."

"They've been terrible! First the accident, then what everyone's been saying."

She waited for me to swallow the hook, but I didn't take the bait, only because somebody else had made a grab for it first and took it hook, line, and sinker. It was Patricia.

"What has everybody been saying?"

"Well, it's not actually what everyone's been saying. It's what I heard Chris had said." Jennifer looked straight at me and her eyes were sparkling. "That you don't think it was an accident. Is that true?"

Now, how do you like that? It's not enough these days in the PR game to help put fires out, it was also to help start them ablaze. And right under my feet, no less. Was she fishing for a commission or what?

Patricia said, "Of course, it was an accident."

Around the table conversations paused and eyes turned. Even the conversation that Frances and Tom were trapped in stopped for a moment.

Jennifer still had her eyes at me. "But you don't believe it was an accident?" She smiled prettily, but she wasn't being pretty. If nobody had been watching, I could've stuffed her under the table — she was no bigger than a sushi roll.

But everybody was watching. And then it hit me. I was being confronted with a choice, and a stark one at that. Was I serious, or wasn't I? I could easily sidestep the whole ordeal and say that I was fine with the accident explanation and appease Patricia and the others and go back to work and everything could go back to the way it was, all except that it would be a lie and Vic would still be dead and whoever killed him would probably get away with it. Or I could stand my ground and confirm what I had said, which wouldn't appease Patricia and the others, and take the heat. Jeff and I had come this evening without any real lever to pry the lid off this mess, Jeff's handshake not withstanding, and hoping something might happen was a pathetic plan to say the least. I deliberated for barely three seconds before realizing I was serious and what came out of my mouth was, "I don't believe Vic was a dope."

The way the Mirandas reacted you'd have thought I killed Vic myself. They all started yapping at once, with Patricia wailing over the noise, "What's he saying? What's he saying?" But Eric's voice was loudest. "The only idiot is you, Chris! Why can't you keep your opinions to yourself? Were you born yesterday?"

That needed a response, so I said, "I may've been born yesterday, but I stayed up all night."

Then the girl in the red dress paid me a compliment. She laughed.

Patricia, in contrast, was not amused. "I think all you're doing is stirring up trouble!"

"I thought I was standing up for Vic."

"So, I'm not! Is that what you're saying?"

"I didn't say that—" But before I could go on, Patricia took the glass full of wine she was holding and tossed it into my face. I should've seen it coming. Patricia was never one to be upstaged.

Then she spun on her heels and took advantage of the room made by those close to the table who had stepped back from the splatter to make her escape. She kept right on going through the crowd of patrons who were watching her every step, with Frances and Tom and Benny and Eric in her wake trying to console her, until she was through the doorway that led to the offices. Exit stage left.

Wine was still dripping down my face. I licked my lips, tasting it. "Unexpectedly bold," I said, "with a spicy finish."

Chapter 6

Now that the excitement was over, I surveyed the damage. My shirt and tie were toast, but my jacket for the most part had weathered the onslaught pretty well. Patrons near the table were standing clear, which was sensible since I was dripping Patricia's wine all over the place. Nobody felt the need to fire any more questions at me about Vic for the moment, which was a relief. Jennifer Kimura, having accomplished whatever her mission was, though I suspected it was purely a bombing raid, had made a quick fade, which was a good thing because I just might've tossed some wine at her myself if she had stuck around.

I reached for the napkins on the table, but before I could there was a shapely hand offering me some. I looked up. It was the girl in the red dress.

"Thanks," I said as I took the napkins and sopped wine off my face and neck.

"You're welcome," she said and smiled, her eyes dancing with amusement. "You looked like you could use a hand."

"I appreciate it."

She glanced down at the wine puddle on the floor she was stepping in.

"Yeah, watch out for that," I said.

She ignored the puddle and put out her hand. "My name's Rosalynd."

I made sure my hand was dry with the napkins before I took hers. "Glad to meet you. I'm Chris—"

"Chris Garrett, I know." Her voice was soft and danced with amusement much like her eyes. "Everyone's been talking about you."

"Talking? About me?"

"Well, not quite talking, more like cursing."

"Ouch."

She smiled. She seemed to think I was funny, so I smiled back.

"That doesn't bother you?" she asked.

I looked down at my shirt and tie. "Sure, I'm bothered."

"But it doesn't change what you think."

"If I had known earlier about all the cursing, I might've lied."

"Somehow, I doubt that."

I shrugged.

Then she asked, "Why do you think it wasn't an accident?"

I had forgotten for a moment she was Eric's girl, and that pulled me up.

"Why do you want to know?"

The change in my tone made her lose the smile. "I was only curious."

"Yeah, I'm curious too."

She didn't shy away. "Why? I suppose it's because you're sticking to such an unpopular opinion." There was a hint of the smile again.

I had missed the smile.

"Opinion. You're right. About all I have is opinion."

"That Vic wasn't a dope."

"Yep, and some little things like the glasses not being on the shelf. But mostly it's my opinion that Vic wasn't an idiot."

"But the deputy who fell in—" She certainly was all caught up with what had happened yesterday.

"He was an idiot."

The smile was back. "That's not a lot to base an opinion on."

I shrugged again.

"But you're still confident you're right," she said.

"Yep."

She noticed some wine still in my hair and dabbed at it with another napkin before it could leak.

"Thanks," I said.

Maybe it was because her smile was so captivating, or

because she was standing so close, but I felt I needed to convince her, too, somehow. So I said, "Look, Vic was no fool. He was one of the top winemakers in the Valley. Him dying like he did, would be like say, a top chef who was chopping carrots accidentally slipped and cut his own throat."

Rosalynd didn't respond. She was looking past me, so I turned and saw across the room near the offices that Eric was beckoning to her.

"I'm being summoned."

"Yeah, you are, aren't you?"

I looked back at her and she had her hand out. "Well, it was nice meeting you, Chris."

I took it. "Nice to meet you too, Rosalynd."

She smiled once more and then headed toward Eric. I watched her go, and I could see across the room that Eric was watching too.

It took me a moment to realize that somebody else was also watching, standing next to me at my elbow. It was Jeff.

"Hubba-hubba." He leered.

"Yeah, she's not hard to look at."

We watched as Rosalynd, having finally reached Eric, retreated with him through the doorway to the offices.

"What's she doing with Knucklehead?"

"Eric?" I gave him a look. "I'm not really sure."

Jeff, I saw, was appraising me. He looked a little amused himself. "Uh-huh. Is that all?"

"Well, she was curious about why I thought it wasn't an accident."

"She might be bird-dogging for Eric. Or for the whole bunch of 'em."

"She might."

"But you're not really sure."

"No. Frances told me she thought Rosalynd was kind of cold and aloof. In her words, 'she doesn't have an emotional bone in her body'."

"An ice queen in a red dress." He wasn't buying it.

"Yeah, I don't buy it either," I said. "She was neither aloof, nor cold."

"No. She was burning the place down. Your ears are still smoking."

I gave him a nod, exhaling loudly.

Nothing juices the tastes buds better than good pre-dinner theater, and I had to admit, Patricia always delivers. That crowd was something to see as it waded into the grub, which was top notch. To start with, there was a risotto with fresh sheep's cheese wrapped in goose prosciutto, then a lamb stew in pea sauce with fried zucchini blossoms filled with mint mousse. Finally, quail baked in a sauterne glaze until the skin crackled, nested on a bed of herb infused faro. Dessert was apple pan dowdy and each course was matched with one of Maverick Cellars' wines.

Benny had pulled me aside just before we sat down to eat and said that we would talk about the incident with Patricia later, but for now, we should just go on with the program as if the tiff never happened, which seemed sensible enough. The Mirandas didn't entirely adopt the 'tiff never happened' position and treated me as if I had a disfiguring disease that was contagious and kept their distance and that included Rosalynd. I don't know if she was of like mind or not, because Eric had her corralled off with the rest of the Mirandas the whole time and she never broke away. There were no more fireworks, which was good because Jeff and I had enough on our hands trying to keep our eyes and ears alert for clues. All in all, it had been a night to remember, for various reasons.

Jeff stayed on after the last of the revelers were shooed out the door and was helping me batten down the hatches. It was getting late and like most memorable parties had spilled over into the next day, and we were helping the catering staff load the last of the tables and chairs into the back of their bobtail, so they might get home tonight at a reasonable hour.

Jeff was hoisting his end of a table we were carrying over the back bumper of the truck.

"So what did we learn?" I asked, groaning as I hoisted my end of the table.

Jeff eased it in next to the other tables and waited until we could rest our muscles before he answered. "We learned your method got better results than mine did."

"Yeah, for some reason, the Mirandas don't like the idea Vic was maybe pushed in."

"Patricia anyway." Then he laughed again thinking about it.

I had to smile too. "She caught me completely flat-footed."

"Her aim was deadly. Right between the eyes, pow!"

"You saw it?"

"Everybody saw it."

"Oh, yeah." I remembered. I then asked, "Who was the most interesting in your opinion?"

"Definitely Patricia. She's got something to hide, or I'm a complete idiot and should be fired."

"Hey, you can't be fired. You're not getting paid for this."

"I'm not getting paid?"

"Not by me."

"Are you getting paid?"

"No."

"What's a matter with us?"

I shrugged. "I blame it on lack of sleep. But I agree with you. We need to find out what Patricia's hiding."

"If she did it, I'll be honest, I'd be disappointed."

"You would?"

"I'd love to throw the cuffs on Eric. That'd be all the pay I'd need."

"He has shown a new found interest in the family business."

"See! I'm telling you Eric's the one, the little rat bastard."

The caterers had the last of the tables and chairs loaded, so Jeff and I got out of their way to let them close up the truck.

"Anybody else?" I asked.

Jeff gave me a look. It took me only a moment to guess what he was thinking.

"The girl in the red dress," I said.

"The girl in the red dress," he repeated.

"Why was she so curious?"

"Why was she with Eric?"

"Poor eye-sight?"

"No. He's not the type that would make me jump the fence," Jeff said. "But he's the type girls go for."

"I know. It's what makes him so hard to take."

"Since she's with Eric, she's automatically suspect."

"Yeah."

Jeff was watching me closely. "What about you? Did you find somebody interesting?"

"Besides who we've touched on?"

He nodded.

I thought about it for a second. "I find Gerry Zacks interesting."

"Zacks, why? He wasn't even here."

"That's why."

So another day and night had come to its end, and Jeff and I, the last two still at Maverick Cellars, locked everything up and called it quits. Then we each headed home. As I finally pulled my pickup into my spot back at Marjorie's and killed the engine, I was yawning so wide and long I nearly unhinged my jaw. But I was mistaken about the day and night being over. As my lights swept into the drive, I caught sight at the curb in front of Marjorie's of a patrol car from the Sheriff's Department, sitting there in the dark. I sat a moment behind the wheel wondering what this was all about, and when I looked back over my shoulder at the patrol car its headlamps flashed on and off. Somebody inside was beckoning. So I got out of my truck and walked over, peering into the driver's window as I did. The dash lights inside lit the face of Sheriff Coulette.

His window was down, and he said, "Get in."

I went around to the passenger's door and he unlocked it for me. I slid in and shut the door.

"Sheriff," I said in greeting.

He nodded. "What the hell're you trying to pull, Garrett."

"Excuse me?"

"You know what I'm talking about. I got a call from Patricia this evening."

Ah, so that was it. "She still upset?"

"What do you think?" But before I could answer, he went on, "Of course I know what you think. Everybody within earshot knows what you think. But I'm more interested in knowing what you think you're pulling."

"It isn't to upset Patricia, if that's what you're asking." Unless she has something to hide about Vic's death, but I kept that to myself.

"Go on."

"Well, isn't it obvious? I think Vic didn't have an accident. I think the whole idea of Vic being that foolish stinks. And it pisses me off to see everybody just accepting it. I want to know why his death isn't being investigated." Maybe I was being a little reckless, talking that way to the Sheriff, but my bedtime was far enough past that in a few hours I'd be getting up again. That's if I got to go to sleep in the first place.

"There's nothing to investigate!" the Sheriff said. "It was

61

an accident."

"You knew Vic. He wasn't a dope."

"Maybe not. But Vic may've gotten careless. You said your-self that everybody including Vic had been working around the clock. I don't like that he's dead any better than you do. He was my sister's husband for Christ's sake! But shit hap-pens. End of story." He could see I wasn't convinced, so he tried another angle. "Let's assume for a moment you're right. It was homicide, and we start an investigation. Who do you think we'd investigate first?"

From his look I could guess the answer already. "Me?"

"That's right. You. You were the last person with Vic before he drowned. Homicide investigators are usually very interested in the last person with the deceased, you, and the first person who finds the body."

"Álvaro."

"Right."

"You don't believe Álvaro or I killed him?"

"I believe it was an accident!" He was getting exasperated. "Listen, I want you to drop this whole thing. You're upsetting my sister. It's hard enough dealing with the loss of her husband without you stirring up more trouble for her. You got that?"

"Or if I don't, you'll sick the police dogs on us."

"Get out of my car!" He wasn't exasperated any longer. He was mad. "Get out!"

I got out of his car. He had the engine turned over and in gear in a split second, and then he roared away. I made sure my feet were out of the way of his tires.

Now what was that all about? If it wasn't so late, and I wasn't so tired I'd put my mind on it, so instead I decided to file it away and I would think about it tomorrow. I headed to my apartment.

When I opened the front door, the phone was ringing. I looked at my watch. It was too frigging dark to read it so I had to find the light switch first. The phone kept ringing. I found it and flipped the light on and looked at my watch. 2:11 am! Who could be calling me at two in the morning? Whoever they were they were persistent, because they weren't calling it quits even after nine or so rings. I made it to the phone and answered. "Hello?"

"Chris?" It was a woman's voice, sort of soft. I thought I recognized it. "Hi, it's Rosalynd." Yep, I did recognize it. "I hope it's not too late to call. I tried you earlier a couple of times."

"Naw, it's fine. I haven't gone to bed yet. What's up?"

"I'm heading back tomorrow afternoon to San Francisco, and I was wondering if you were free for lunch."

"Lunch?"

"If you're free."

"Lunch?" Yeah, my brain was short-circuiting.

"That's right." I thought I caught a bit of amusement in her voice.

What was this all about? Was she asking me out — or was she trying to pump me for more information? If I wasn't so beat I might've known better what was going on.

"Uh," I exhaled, trying to think. "No, I'm afraid I'll be in up to my eyeballs at Maverick Cellars."

"How about breakfast, then?"

"Again, up to my eyeballs at Maverick Cellars."

"When do you start working tomorrow?"

"You mean, today?"

"Sorry, today." There was that amusement again.

"In around four hours."

"Good God," she said. Then, "Well, how about before that? There's got to be someplace we could get a cup of coffee."

She definitely was persistent.

I offered, "How about the Farmers Market? We might even find a croissant along with that coffee."

"That's perfect."

"You know where it is?"

"No."

"Then listen up," I said. There were actually two different ones in St. Helena held at different locations on different days, and I had to remember which one it was that was on for tomorrow, I mean today, and then fill her in. I sent the cogs and wheels in my brain spinning once more and told her how to find it and we agreed on a time. Five-thirty. I don't remember saying, 'good-bye' before I hung up the phone, which was poor manners if I didn't, but it only worried me for two minutes. That's how long it took to navigate my way to bed, to set the alarm on my clock radio, to strip off my clothes, to slide between the sheets and to lay my head on my pillow. It took only three seconds more to slip into oblivion.

Chapter 7

FEELING RESTED AND refreshed after a whole three hours of sleep, I joyfully hopped out of bed raring to go. Okay, so I wasn't very joyful, nor was I feeling very rested or refreshed, but I did get into a sitting position on the edge of the mattress without too much groaning and complaining. Looking at the clock radio, I had a leisurely twelve minutes to shower and shave and dress before I had to be out the door. That meant I could sit there for another fifteen seconds with my eyes closed and not throw my schedule too far out of whack, so I did, and it did wonders. I actually got to my feet and got to the bathroom and under some scalding hot water and started shaving. I finished that, not hacking my face up too much, and I got into an equally scalding shower for a relaxing four minutes.

Then I dug around and found some appropriate clothes for another day at the office, remembered to brush my teeth and headed for Crane Park with my hair still wet to where today's Farmers Market was being held. I was ahead of schedule a minute twenty seconds, which should've made me happy, but all I could think about was that I could've slept in.

It was early, apparently even for the farmers. The market wasn't open yet for business as I pulled in and parked, but most of them were already setting up, hoisting awnings and signs and positioning crates of fruits and vegetables. The sky was lit up but the sun hadn't yet cleared the Vaca Range and the Valley floor where the Market was being held was still somewhat foggy. I had sat in my truck only for a few minutes before a Mercedes convertible pulled in next to me with the top up and I saw it was Rosalynd. When she smiled at me, I felt my stomach lurch, which was not a good sign. For all I knew, she had nefarious motives, and I should be more suspicious, but she was so damn good looking.

I hopped out and so did she, and I saw she wasn't wearing a red dress like last night, but had switched to denim pants and a light sports shell to keep out the morning chill. She didn't look like she had only slept for three hours.

"Good morning," she said.

"Good morning." We shook hands, and I said, "We're a little early. But I think we might find a cup of coffee if we try. They usually have an espresso stand set up."

She nodded, and we set off.

"I hope you're not annoyed with me, calling so late."

"Naw, forget it. That's the only time I'm usually home."

"I wanted to talk to you more at dinner, but it didn't work out."

"Yeah, things got somewhat complicated, didn't they?"

She smiled. "They sure did."

We walked down the stalls being set up and nodded and said "hello" to those vendors who happened to notice us and look up. Ahead, where the espresso stand stood I saw a number of people gathered there, so was still hopeful we would find a cup available and was I ever needing one.

Then Rosalynd said, "Hey, isn't that your friend?"

I looked closer and of the people gathered there holding cups of coffee steaming in the morning air were two deputies from the Sheriff's Department. One of them was Jeff. What the heck was he doing here?

"Yeah," I laughed incredulously.

"I thought I recognized him from the dinner last night."

I looked at Rosalynd. She wasn't only persistent she was perceptive.

I must've had a questioning look on my face because she said, "I remember you talking to him."

"Oh." She had had her eye on me last night more than I realized.

"Did you know he'd be here?" she asked.

"No clue."

As we approached, Jeff was watching us. He didn't look surprised to see us, only suspicious.

"I thought you'd still be in bed," I said to him.

"I am. I gotta be dreaming." He was looking straight at Rosalynd.

"I know the feeling." When he looked back at me I said, "I don't think you've met Rosalynd Warder. Rosalynd, this is Jeff Beckwell."

They shook hands and said the pleasant things that people say when they first meet, and Jeff introduced us to his partner in uniform and everybody traded more handshakes.

The espresso stand was in full swing and I motioned to Rosalynd and said, "What will you have?"

"Latte, please."

I ordered one for her and asked for a large cup of regular java for myself.

While we waited, Rosalynd smiled at Jeff and asked, "Do Chris and you come here often?"

"To the Farmers Market?" Jeff asked back, skipping any innuendo implied or otherwise and when she nodded said, "Oh, yeah! We shop here all the time. We love this place, don't we Chris?"

I didn't remember ever professing my love, but he was roping me in on wherever he was going with this, so I nodded. "I sure do."

"We're gourmets," he said with a straight face. At her look of incredulity, he admonished, "Oh, we love to cook. Love it! Actually we're amateur chefs. Go ahead," he said to me, "tell her the last thing you whipped up. Go on, tell her."

"Jeff," I stammered, "I've been so busy lately I haven't had time to cook. I've barely had time to eat. I've been living on frozen dinners."

Rosalynd looked back at Jeff for a response, and with no way out he sheepishly admitted, "Yeah, me too."

Our coffees were ready so I paid for them and we took them to the service tray and got the right blend of milk and sweetener. Jeff and his fellow deputy had to clock in, so when our coffees were to our liking we followed them to their squad car nearby and said our good-byes. What I wanted to do, since he was here was to take him to the side and tell him about the visit I had from Sheriff Coulette and get his take on the matter, but I was cautious about bringing it up in the present company. So as Jeff climbed behind the wheel, I stopped him with a look instead and said, "We need to talk later."

He gave a quick glance at Rosalynd before nodding. "Okay. I'll call you."

"All right."

I stepped back and Rosalynd and I waved and watched them pull out of the lot.

As we did, she said, "Your friend is very playful."

"Jeff?" I laughed. "He's a nut."

"But there's something else. I noticed it when we first met. Something darker below the surface, more menacing."

I had to hand it to her she definitely was perceptive.

"A lot of people don't catch that side of him. But you're right. You wouldn't want to get on Jeff's bad side."

"I can believe that." She took a small sip of her coffee, thinking for a bit. Then she asked, "Does Jeff think it was an accident?"

"No. He's with me on that."

"Are you worried that you two are the only ones concerned?"

"I wouldn't say we're the only ones concerned. Not after last night."

Rosalynd smiled.

"The Mirandas seemed very concerned to me," I said.

She nodded, and sipped at her coffee again. "I suppose you're right."

So I tried my coffee and it was of course molten lava and I scalded my lips. I should've taken heed of the stinging heat coming through the sides of the paper cup and saved myself from pain, but I was short of sleep and craving caffeine. If the pain hadn't jolted me awake, it would've been Rosalynd's next question.

"What're you planning to do next?"

I gave her a look and said, "Is that why you wanted to see me?"

She looked amused again. "You're very suspicious. But yes, that was one of the reasons I called you. Maybe not the main reason, but one of them." She did something with her eyes and my stomach flopped again. "You may not believe me, because you're so suspicious, but I agree with you and your friend. Something's not right about Vic's death, and I'm curious to see how everything will come out."

She was right about me. She seemed truthful enough, but she also might be molten lava like my coffee and I wasn't prepared to swallow it.

"Do you have a plan?" she asked again.

"Uh, no."

"You're not just saying that? You really have no idea what to do?"

"Oh, I'm full of ideas," and left it at that.

"But you won't share them with me?"

"Let's say, I don't want to share them with Eric."

"Because you suspect Eric is involved?"

"I don't know."

"And if I said, 'you didn't have to worry about me,' you'd say—"

"I'd say, 'we'll see.'"

She was doing that thing with her eyes again. "Still suspicious."

I hoped steam wasn't coming from my ears. As a distraction, I decided to check my watch and saw that I'd have to get to the winery soon, and Rosalynd caught on.

"You gotta go?"

"Yeah," I sighed. "Shall we start back?"

"Okay."

Then I remembered, "I promised you a croissant to go with the coffee." I was looking for the bakery vendor.

She touched my arm and said, "You can get me one, next time."

"A rain check?"

"It doesn't have to be raining."

Yep. Molten Lava.

After saying goodbye to Rosalynd, I made for the Maverick

Cellars Fitness Center and my early morning-midday-late afternoon-early evening total body workout. Who needs a gym with weights and barbells when you can bowl barrels and heave hoses all day? Actually, I had to get serious about what to do with all of Tony Picozzi's fruit. He would have the pickers out tomorrow bright and early and from his estimates, and his estimates were usually accurate, I already knew I didn't have enough tank space to handle all the grapes coming in, even though I had emptied two tanks yesterday and fortunate or not had a third tank available. Vic and I had talked about what we'd do if such a problem arose. If the harvest wasn't too large we could rent extra tanks until we could barrel it down, or we could send the overflow to Bakerwood Winery. From Tony's estimates, and my own for that matter, we could go either way, the first choice being slightly less expensive than doing a full custom crush at Bakerwood Winery. On the other hand, Bakerwood Winery had plenty of space available, and unlike Maverick Cellars, the winemaking equipment was brand new and state of the art with all the latest gadgets and gizmos, and I was itching to give it a test drive, much like a car nut would a new Ferrari.

As it turned out, I didn't have to make the choice, because Benny did it for me. He was at the winery when I got there and said he had talked last night at the dinner with Matt Bakerwood of Bakerwood Winery and they were all set for us. I just had to go over there with a load of barrels and help coordinate. So that's what I did all morning. After getting the trucking company we work with to send over a flatbed and driver for us, Álvaro and I loaded barrels. I had been expecting Benny to take me to task for the tiff with the Mirandas, but he didn't bring it up, so I didn't bring it up either.

I took Álvaro with me in my truck and we followed the flatbed carrying our barrels over to Bakerwood Winery and pulled around back to the crush pad where some of the cellar help were busy with chores. As we got out, both of us caught on immediately that something was wrong at the winery. It was Halleran, Bakerwood Winery's cellar master, who was charging around in a panic, shouting, "That sonofabitch! That sonofabitch!" He had a long pole and was at the fermentation vats, which were the kind that had removable lids and were perfect for doing manual punchdowns. He was poking the pole through the cap of fermenting grape skins probing for what may lie underneath. I felt a jolt to my nervous system when it dawned on me what he was probing for.

"That sonofabitch!" Halleran moved to a new vat and began his probing all over again. "I always knew this would happen. I always knew — the stupid sonofabitch!"

The rest of the cellar help were just watching, and I noticed a Latino worker near us washing down the pad with a water hose. Álvaro asked him in Spanish what was up, and the cellar worker laughed. I didn't think that was appropriate if what I thought was happening was really happening.

He shut off his hose so we could come closer and being careful that Halleran didn't catch on he confided, "He is looking for his brother." Then he laughed again, clearly amused by the whole situation.

"That's nothing to laugh at," I said.

"You do not understand." He couldn't stop snickering, "His brother — he is not drowned. He is in town drinking at Harvey's!"

Then the rest of it came out, slowly through more snickers about how every Friday, the missing brother would come to work and punch in and when Halleran wasn't looking, he'd sneak off to the bar and be gone all day, but still drawing a paycheck. Everybody knew this had been going on for some time, all except for Halleran. Only today, the cellar master for some reason went looking for his brother and when he couldn't find him had assumed the worst.

"We will tell Halleran, but not yet," said the worker. "This is too good."

It was cruel, but it also was funny, especially since Halleran could be a horse's ass and deserved it. Álvaro and I stood back and enjoyed the spectacle for a bit, and I was struck by how Vic dying like he did was messing with people's heads not only at Maverick Cellars but across the whole Valley, especially if Halleran jumping to the wrong conclusion was any example. One thing was definite — the cellar master wouldn't live this down for a while. The workers under him would make sure of that. As for the missing brother, Halleran would probably kill him.

Álvaro and I headed for the office to locate Matt, and when we got there we found him at his desk on the phone. I knocked lightly at the opened door to get his attention and he waved us in. Matt Bakerwood used to work for Vic and

Benny at Maverick Cellars as Vic's assistant winemaker, the job I had taken on after he had left to start his own winery business, and I had watched his progress with keen interest ever since.

At the moment Matt wasn't enjoying himself. He looked frazzled like most people do during crush, and I figured out from what I could hear from his end of the phone conversation that he was dealing with a barrel manufacturer who was demanding money up front or Matt wouldn't be getting any of the wine barrels he had ordered. Matt was up out of his chair pacing one moment, then sitting back down shuffling through papers scatters over his desk trying to reason that that wasn't how things were done, it was always payment on delivery, but I could tell he was losing the argument. They had him, literally over a barrel. Companies usually don't change their payment policies unless they felt they were dealing with somebody who might have trouble paying them back. Obviously, they figured Matt was a bad risk, and I wondered why. Was Bakerwood Winery in financial difficulty? I knew he was selling out every year all the wine he was producing, or at least that was what I heard from him anyway. Finally in disgust Matt gave in and hung up the phone. He ran his hands through his hair exhaling loudly, and looked at us. "Frigging vultures," he said. Then he was out of his chair again greeting us warmly and shaking our hands.

I motioned toward the phone and asked, "Having some trouble?"

"Naw, just a bunch of bullshit." He waved it away. "So how

goes your morning, fellas?"

"Better than your Cellar Master's at the moment."

"What's that?" He hadn't heard about the commotion going on outside.

"Halleran. He's out there searching the vats with a pole."

Álvaro snickered, "He thinks his brother fell in and drowned when he was not looking."

Matt snorted. "Knowing Halleran's brother, he's probably just drinking down at Harvey's."

"They say that's where he is," I said.

"Figures." He pointed at a couple of chairs so we each took a seat. Then, he plopped down on his chair again and picked up a pen to fiddle with. After a moment fiddling with the pen, he said, "So, you don't swallow the accident, huh?"

It was a blunt question, so I thought it deserved a blunt answer. "No. Do you?"

Matt ignored my question and looked at Álvaro. "What do you think about Vic dying like that?"

Álvaro shrugged, but then he glanced at me and said, "Seemed like a stupid way to die."

I hadn't asked Álvaro what he thought about Vic's accident, but it was gratifying to know his thoughts ran similar to my own.

Matt nodded and looked again at me. "A united front."

"You don't agree?"

"Naw, I didn't say that."

"How do you think he died?"

He fiddled some with the pen before saying, "I don't know."

He got up out of his chair to pace and I wondered if something more was bothering him.

"You know anybody who might've wanted to give Vic a push?"

He gave me an eye and for a second I thought he was going to say, 'yes' but instead he just said, "You want to know what I think? I think you're taking on a lot of grief. You got any reason to think Vic was pushed?"

"Vic wasn't a dope."

"Besides that?"

"No."

He gave his chair a look and I thought he was going to take a seat again, but he decided not to and remained on his feet. "Telling everybody Vic was murdered, now that's stupid."

I shrugged it off.

"You should watch what you say around this Valley," he said. "Take my advice. Never make people think you're a troublemaker. It's the surest way to get a bad reputation. And in this Valley, reputation is everything."

"You're probably right," I said.

"I am right! You could find yourself out of a job."

"Okay, you're right," I agreed, trying not to make trouble.

"This could all come back and bite you in the ass."

"Yeah, I'm aware of that," I said, smiling. "I don't have much ass left after last night."

He thought about it for a moment and smiled too. Then all of us were chuckling about what had happened with Patricia and the wine.

"C'mon," he said. "Let me show you around."

After getting our barrels unloaded and jotting down everything we needed Matt to know about how Bakerwood Winery would be handling and processing our fruit for us and giving him a heads up on when to expect us tomorrow morning, Álvaro and I headed back to Maverick Cellars. On our way, we stopped in at the local grocery and bought lunch for our crew, a mess of turkey sandwiches and assorted styles of chips — this being the Napa Valley, not all chips were potato anymore, nor did people expect them to be that way — so the crew got carrot and rutabaga and blue turnip and sweet potato (which for the record were my favorite), and when we finally got back it was a little after twelve.

The crew knew beforehand that we were bringing lunch and moments after we arrived word spread and soon everybody was gathered in the winery kitchen digging in. Tony Picozzi happened to be there as well, wanting to talk details about the harvest tomorrow, so he got a sandwich too.

"You got them with everything?" Tony was unwrapping his sandwich.

I nodded. "I told them to drag 'em through the garden."

"Good." Tony had his sandwich opened and seemed satisfied. Then he found the mint chocolate they had also slipped into each order, and then I knew he was satisfied. "Paisano!" he said grinning.

There was a big table that the kitchen staff used for food preparations and most everybody found a spot around it. Álvaro was looking through cupboards and then through the refrigerator, but he was having no success finding whatever he was after.

"Where are the chilies?"

I had taken a bite of sandwich and it tasted fine to me without further doctoring and after swallowing said, "Why do Mexicans put chili peppers on everything they eat?"

Álvaro was eyeing some Thai fish sauce he had found in the back of the fridge and was reading the label of ingredients. "Not all Mexicans like chilies," he said. "Remember Hector, at the harvest picnic. He cannot stand hot chilies." He had the lid off the fish sauce and poured a healthy portion over his turkey sandwich, then he paused, "Come to think of it, he is Salvadoran."

Tony said to me, his mouth full of turkey, "We need to talk."

"Okay, shoot."

"No. You need to talk with Benny first."

"Is he here?"

Tony nodded and took another bite before saying, "In the office. He asked to see you when you got back. After you talk with him, you talk with me, capiche?"

I nodded, and hoped Tony would be done with his food by then. I loved seafood, but not that kind of see-food. I pushed my lunch aside and got up and grabbed another sandwich and some chips in case Benny wanted lunch and started from the kitchen. Álvaro had cleaned up his sandwich with the Thai-sauce concoction in nothing flat and was reading again from the sauce bottle and grimacing. Before I made the door,

I heard him say, "That was just horrible."

Benny was standing at the window in his office as I came though the doorway. His back was to me, but his stance was rigid, and at once I knew something was up and it wasn't going to be pleasant. He was staring out at our vineyard and at the Valley that lay beyond, which stretched clear to the Mayacamas Range. He had a newspaper gripped tightly in his hands. I knocked gently at the door, and he turned and saw me.

I held up the sandwich. "Hungry?"

He said, "You can put it on the desk."

I did.

Then Benny glanced down at the newspaper he held tight and after a moment offered it to me. "You better read this."

I took the paper from him and saw it was today's San Francisco Sentinel. My eyes swept the headlines, but it didn't take more than a second to find what Benny wanted me to see. It was half way down the page on the left side: "Winemaker's Death May Not Be Accidental."

Chapter

8

AFTER GIVING THE article a quick read I should've been annoyed. The gist was that the officials inquiring into Vic's death had been hasty and had stopped the investigation too soon, which was fine. That had been my intention all along to get the officials to do more inquiring, but the paper had used me to do it and really hung my ass out there. I was referred to three times, by name. It's one thing to stand up for your position when challenged, but it was quite another to be used by whoever wrote the article as a club to flog the Sheriff's Department with. On the other hand, I had made the choice already to take the heat, and so what if it was getting hotter? I wasn't about to back down now. Jeff and I were looking for some way to stir things up and this would certainly help. At the dinner last night there were only a couple hundred people, the reach of the Sentinel was easily half a million.

Benny said, "Did you talk with the press?"

"No."

"Are you sure? You look like their main source of information!"

"They didn't get it from me." Which wasn't entirely true, I hadn't talked with anybody from the paper, but as I reread the article again this time more carefully I might as well have. I had made my opinions known in public more than once already and for the most part the reporter had done his or her homework and had me down correctly, but beyond that there wasn't much new. Figures. "Had to be somebody at last night's dinner," I said. "We invite anybody who works for the paper?"

"Who knows?" Benny went to his desk and sat down. "They didn't have to work for the paper, just know somebody who did and pass it along."

"Has Patricia seen it?"

"I don't know." He rubbed at his eyes. "She hasn't called, but when she does—"

"She's liable to chuck some wine at somebody."

"Uh-huh," he wasn't entirely amused and was still at his eyes, rubbing them good like he was trying to rub out the image of Patricia reacting like she was apt to do, but it was no use. When he finally looked up at me his bloodshot eyes were good and swollen. "And she will see this!"

"Yeah."

"It won't be long before everybody has seen this!"

I nodded.

"Chris, you've got to watch what you say in public. You're in charge now and people are listening to you. You can't go off half-cocked anymore. It'll hurt Maverick Cellars."

"Hurting Maverick Cellars was never my intention—"

"I realize that. Vic dying like he did, well," his jaw came loose at the thought of Vic, but he got it under control and said, "it created a lot of hoopla that's not going away overnight. But we can keep from making things worse. We're in the middle of the largest expansion we've ever taken on, with new vineyards beginning to bear and the last thing we need right now is more bad publicity. You can see that?"

I could and conceded the point.

"I want you to promise me that under no condition will you talk with the press about Vic's death. Now," he put up a palm, "I know how you feel about the matter, and I even sympathize, but Maverick Cellars cannot afford it! Will you promise me?"

What damage the paper had done or not done to Maverick Cellars I hadn't a clue, and frankly, it was too soon to tell one way or another in my opinion, but I could see no advantage in telling Benny that, so I promised. Any hard facts that may turn up in the future would more than likely get to the press anyway, whether I filled them in on it or not, and I hadn't filled them in on it directly in the first place. Even so, Benny pressed me further on how serious this could affect our business and I had to assure him twice more that the press would get nothing more from me, 'cross my heart and hope to die,' before he was satisfied. "And no more public announcements!" I shrugged that off too and promised him again.

Benny's anxiety about how much Maverick Cellars had riding on this new venture got me thinking, though, about his other partner and business angel Gerry Zacks. "Whatever happened to Gerry?" I asked. "I thought he was brought on board for just this sort of problem."

Benny gave me a look. "It's never that simple."

"I suppose not," I said. "Is he in town? I thought Zacks would show at last night's dinner, but if he did I missed him."

Benny kept his eyes on me for a moment. "I don't know what happened to Gerry. I thought he'd be there too. Strange. He usually comes to that sort of thing." Then he waved it away. "He's probably out of town on business or out of the country. He's busy like that, nothing to worry about. He'll turn up."

"You mind if I try calling him?"

"You know, that's a good idea," Benny said, feeling in his pockets for I assumed a pen and paper. "We're ready to start harvesting his fruit. He might want to hear from his new winemaker."

So Benny got me Zack's number and having gotten the problem with the newspaper settled, took up his sandwich and asked how things were shaping up at Bakerwood Winery. I filled him in. We went over details about tomorrow's harvest and how many fruit bins we had available and how many we'd need, which if my calculations were correct would mean that we'd be on the short side, but all that meant was we would have to take some of the first bins we emptied back to Tony and his pickers as soon as possible. I made a note of it so I wouldn't forget, which made me remember something else I wanted to ask Benny about.

"How is Matt these days?"

"All right, I suppose." Then he paused, his sandwich half-way to his mouth. "Why do you ask?"

"When I was over there this morning, I got the impression his business wasn't doing that well."

Benny set his lunch aside without taking a bite and leaned back in his chair and regarded me, gauging I suspected how much he should let on about Matt Bakerwood's financial troubles. "Matt has built himself a beautiful facility over there," he said. "He has also built up a lot of overhead. All that new equipment you've been drooling over doesn't come cheap."

I was nodding, having already put it together. "That's why we're custom crushing with him."

Benny smiled. "Matt was a good employee for us when he worked here, just like you are now, Chris. I thought the least we could do was throw a little business his way. Help him out of a tough spot." It made sense and I should've expected something like that from Benny. I smiled back.

Benny got at his sandwich, so I left him to his lunch and found Tony still in the kitchen and got everything straightened out with him for tomorrow morning, telling him about the bin shortage, and he told me about how he and Vic years ago had to run twelve crumby broken down bins back and frigging forth twenty or thirty goddamn times just to get all the fruit in from one vineyard block. Compared to that, this would be a frigging cakewalk.

I hoped Tony was right because the rest of that day wasn't much of a cakewalk, more like a sprint — a long series of muscle-tiring chores with sporadic interruptions from my cell phone, mostly from people who had seen the article in the paper and had had the sudden urge to touch base. What they actually had had was the sudden urge to get any news that I happened to have that I hadn't thought fit to print. I had little success explaining that I hadn't talked with anybody in the press in the first place, so therefore I had nothing more to tell, and none of them had anything worthwhile to tell me so both sides hung up unsatisfied. One interesting point — there had been no reaction from any of the Mirandas, which I realized after about the fifth call or so that I was fully expecting word of some kind from at least one of them and the stomach clenching I was doing after each new ring was me anticipating a blow. Well, the blow never came. Not that my guts told me one of them was guilty. I knew nothing that had me leaning one way or another on that. I hadn't heard back from Gerry Zacks either, even though I had called his number three different times throughout the day leaving messages to call me. I did get a call from Jeff though like he promised and we decided to meet at my place after work, and so it was a little after seven that evening when I pulled my truck into my space in front of Marjorie's and saw Jeff's Jeep parked in the same spot the

Sheriff's patrol car had occupied last night.

Jeff was leaning against the post railing in front of the main house listening to Marjorie, who was on the porch dressed in exercise tights and had a duffel bag at her feet.

As I approached, Marjorie was saying "—and I said to her, 'What do you mean nobody's talking about me behind my back?'"

Jeff laughed.

"I mean, the way I threw myself at him, talk about brazen," she was going on, apparently filling Jeff in on her latest love interest. "I told you how good looking he was, well, later he calls me on the phone and all he wants to do is talk and talk and talk, and that would be fine if he talked about something I was interested in."

"Like yourself for instance," Jeff said.

"Exactly!" she said. "Well after five minutes I'm bored to tears, and he goes on for like an hour! So I get fed up and I tell him not to call me anymore unless he's calling to ask me out on a date."

"Did he ask you out?" Jeff asked.

"Yes!" she said in triumph. "We're meeting for drinks tomorrow night!" Then she looked up and saw me standing there. "Chris. Did you make it home at all last night?"

"Yeah, apparently after you went to sleep," I said. "And I left this morning before you got up."

"Honey, that's no way to live. You look terrible."

I had to agree with her, the 'no way to live' part, not the 'looking terrible' part. I've mentioned before how much sleep

I usually need not to look like damaged goods. I ran my hand through my hair in response and grinned at Jeff who was holding the brown bag of Chinese takeout he had said he was bringing. He hadn't slept much himself last night and looked as tired as I felt.

"Well, I'm late for dance practice," Marjorie said grabbing up her duffel, and in a burst of energy rushed down the steps. She caught me in the middle of a yawn. "Try to get some sleep tonight," she said. "I worry about you sometimes." Then waved. "Bye, you two."

We waved back with half her energy, though she was probably double our age and watched her quickly hop into her car and zip off to wherever her dance group did their practicing.

Jeff held up the brown bag, nodding knowingly. "See that grease leaking through?"

I nodded. "The sign of quality."

"I spared no expense."

"The smell has me drooling like some half-starved hound. C'mon, let's eat." I motioned him toward my place and we headed inside.

The takeout was quickly unloaded onto my coffee table in the living room, and I grabbed a bottle opener from the kitchen for the Tsingtaos he brought with the food. We immediately started digging in.

"What's on the menu?"

"Let's see," Jeff said, taking a sip of his beer and opening the first container, "rice."

"Always a good choice."

"I thought so." Then he opened some others. "General Tso's Chicken, some eggrolls, Dragon Fire Shrimp."

"Álvaro would love that one."

Jeff glanced at the one I was fingering, "That's Shanghai Shoe."

"S-H-O-E, shoe?"

He nodded.

"Something must've gotten lost in translation."

"No, see those tiny dumplings? They're little shoes."

I looked, but I wasn't buying it. "They are not," I said.

Jeff just laughed. You had to watch him closely. You never knew when he might be pulling your leg.

"What about this?" I said, getting another container opened.

"Is it mostly vegetables?"

"Yep."

"That's, The Three Happiness."

"Only three?"

"Well, you know what they say about too much happiness — makes you fat, dumb and lazy — and from what I saw in the paper today, I thought it best we stay thin, quick witted and energetic."

"Good thinking. You saw the article?"

"Yeah, the rotted bastards. I'm assuming you didn't talk with anybody."

"I had nothing to do with it," I said.

"The bastards. They might as well have painted a bulls-eye on your back!"

I shrugged, not really concerned.

Jeff stopped eating and was staring at me, frowning, and I realized he was really mad about this.

"I'm actually pleased the paper got hold of it," I said. "Maybe somebody in the Sheriff's Department will start taking Vic's death more seriously."

Jeff was still staring. "We're still assuming somebody did Vic in, right? If that somebody gets the idea you're becoming a real danger, and if that somebody knows you like I do, it's not just an idea, that somebody just might decide some night to shove you into a wine vat or off a cliff! You ever think of that?"

"That's why I got you, to watch my back for me."

"Uh-huh." He certainly was mad, and I was touched.

"I'm really not that worried."

"You should be!"

I decided to change the subject. "Guess who paid me a visit last night."

"I already know."

"You do?"

"Yeah, and they're probably responsible for the article in the paper."

"Sheriff Coulette?"

"That's who paid you a visit?"

"Who did you think it was?"

"We can skip that for a moment. The Sheriff—"

"Yeah, he was out front waiting for me. In the dark."

"What did he want?"

"Same as everybody else. He wanted me to shut up about what I thought of the accident. Or he'd sick the police dogs on me and Álvaro."

"He give any hint why he was pressuring you?"

"He said it was on account of Patricia." I took him over everything that had happened, and at the end, Jeff was nodding.

"I know a couple people who might know something. Interesting. I'll look into this. I'm pretty sure I can, without stirring up more dust."

I nodded. "You think Sheriff Coulette planted the story in the paper?"

"No. Purposely giving his department a black eye? Hardly. I thought you were talking about your new girlfriend."

"Rosalynd?" I smiled. "You think she was responsible for the article?"

"She's the only person we know from San Francisco. She could've done it. Why else was she pumping you for information?"

I thought about it for a moment, but honestly didn't know. I still hadn't pegged her yet. "If I were to guess, I'd say the culprit was Jennifer Kimura. She has contacts with the press. It's what she does for a living, and the way she acted at the party, I wouldn't put it past her."

"All right then, explain this morning."

"Rosalynd called me after I talked with the Sheriff."

"That was like two in the morning!"

"She'd been trying to get me for a while. I had my cell

phone off."

"Uh-huh. What did she want?"

"Same as before. She's curious about Vic's accident, and what we're up to about it."

It was clear what Jeff thought of that.

"I know," I said. "I haven't forgotten whose girlfriend she really is."

Jeff was still eyeing me.

"By the way," I said. "The funeral's tomorrow at one o'clock."

He reacted like most people do at the thought of going to a funeral only that wasn't what it was that was bothering him. "I suppose I'll have to wear a tie and jacket."

I smiled.

We still hadn't opened all the Chinese food. "What's in the big box?"

"Ah." Jeff's eyes gleamed. "Princess Woo's Seven Secret Desires."

It didn't sound much like food to me. I gave it a stir with some chopsticks. "From the looks of it, her secret's safe."

"That's why I ordered it. Thought we might tease out the mystery."

So we both gave the dish a taste, and though we both teased the heck out of it, neither of us could make any head-way on the mystery.

Offhand I said, "You'd think one of Princess Woo's secret desires would've been General Tso's chicken."

The gag caught Jeff off guard, and he nearly choked on his

Dragon Fire Shrimp. I laughed too, and it took awhile before either of us calmed down enough to eat anymore.

Jeff dug the last container out. "Don't forget this."

"What is it?"

"Hello Kitty soup."

I was skeptical. "Now, you made that up."

Jeff chuckled and admitted, "Yeah, I did. It's Egg Drop Soup."

Chapter 9

THE NEXT MORNING on my way to Bakerwood Winery, I stopped at our vineyard to check on Tony's progress. Tony's picking crew had begun late last night and had picked fruit by lamp light clear through until morning. A bin full of grapes can heat up pretty quickly if left too long in the hot sun, so it was preferable to pick at night when there was no danger. That way, the grapes, having been cooled down by the night air, came into the winery much more stable.

Even though the sun was up, it was still cold especially this early in the morning with the dew rising, and I met up with Tony and his crew still picking in the vineyard and inspected the fruit piling up in the bins. I pulled out some leaves that inadvertently had gotten tossed in with the clusters and tasted some of the berries. Tony came over to hear my verdict.

"Fantastic," I said, savoring the flavor. I was getting none of the greener unripe qualities that were coming through before. The extra couple of days on the vine especially with the heat we were getting in the late afternoon had certainly helped the maturity.

"You should have tasted the fruit when Galbraith had it." Tony was making a face. "Then you would really be impressed."

"Bad, huh?"

"The worst. But the potential was there, if you knew what to look for."

"You recommended buying this place, didn't you Tony?"

"Vic knew how good it was, but yeah, I told them. But it still wouldn't have happened without Zacks. Zacks had the money. You need lots of money to do anything in this Valley anymore."

That was definitely true.

"Well, the fruit looks great," I said.

"And tastes even better!" Tony shoved some grapes into his mouth.

I did likewise, and then said, "You know, I thought Gerry would be out here making a nuisance of himself. Have you heard from him lately?"

Tony shook his head and spit out some seeds. "Nope."

"Neither have I. I tried calling on the phone, but haven't reached him. Figured he wouldn't miss this, being his first vintage."

Tony just shrugged.

A flatbed truck nearby was already loaded with bins and the driver was tying them down, so I went over and climbed up and inspected the fruit. Everything looked fine.

Then Tony still with the pickers yelled across the rows of vines at me, "You heading back?"

"Yeah," I yelled.

"Don't forget to send us more bins!"

I said I wouldn't forget, waved goodbye, hopped into my truck and followed the flatbed to Bakerwood Winery.

Álvaro was already at Bakerwood Winery working with Matt's Cellar Master, Halleran, setting things up when I arrived with the fruit. I joined them and we exchanged good mornings, but before they got back to it, Álvaro winked at me and said offhand, "Hey Halleran, I forgot to ask. Have you found your brother yet?"

Halleran snarled, "Go to hell!" And turned his back on us.

"He's a little touchy this morning," I said to Álvaro.

Álvaro grinned. "Of course, Halleran is usually touchy, so it is hard to tell."

"Also true," I said.

Then Álvaro snickered. "I hear he is catching hell from everybody."

Halleran, his shoulders hunched up under the strain of playing the fool yesterday, had marched over to retrieve the must pump we'd be using to push the fruit once crushed by the destemmer-crusher into the tanks. If he'd just swallow some of his pride and laugh at himself along with everybody else, the whole event would be a lot less painful for him. After all, you'd think he'd be happy his brother wasn't drowned.

The fruit bins taken off the truck by forklift would be dumped into the destemmer-crusher, a large machine with a set of rollers that squeezed the clusters of berries as they dropped through, while inside a spinning drum perforated with holes caught up the stems and allowed the grapes to continue through to a catch basin below. The separated stems exited out the end and fell into another bin for composting later. The whole process wasn't anything as harsh as the word *crush* made it out to be. The idea was to handle the grapes as gently as possible and to not release too much tannin into the finished wine, which ripping and crushing the skins and seeds would certainly do, making the wine taste hard and unfriendly. Winemakers usually liked as many intact berries as possible, which was also my preference, and I should get exactly what I wanted from Bakerwood Winery's destemmer-crusher which compared to some I've seen was a Cadillac, or rather since it was made in Germany, eine Mercedes.

"So this is Galbraith's fruit," I heard Matt Bakerwood say behind me. Having noticed our arrival, he had joined us and was looking at the flatbed full of bins with his hands on his hips. He was smirking. "I didn't expect you'd be making bulk wine."

"Ouch," I said.

"I meant the grapes, not your ability, Chris."

I knew the grapes had been crappy in the past from what

Tony had told me, but I didn't want to let Matt off so easily, so I said, "What's wrong with the grapes?"

"Probably nothing," he said, and started around the truck to watch the truck driver loosening the ropes holding down the bins. "Now that Tony's on top of things."

I followed him around the truck.

Matt looked like he was going to help the driver with the ropes, but then decided the driver had it covered. Then he climbed up and took a cluster of grapes out of a bin and tasted them. He glanced at me, seeing I was still with him and said, "This fruit's not bad."

I shrugged and smiled. "Did Maverick Cellars have a lot of problems with Galbraith?"

"I remember the fruit was crap. Galbraith was a rotten farmer."

"Vic must've been pleased about that."

Matt smiled. "Yeah, I remember Vic and Galbraith going round and round over the shit he tried to push on us."

"He and Vic didn't get along, huh?"

Matt lost his smile and gave me a look. "No they didn't." His eyes narrowed. "You still looking for somebody with a motive?"

I shrugged.

He jumped down off the flatbed. "You're wasting your time."

"More than likely," I said. "They ever come to blows?"

"Not that I know of."

Matt started off again around the truck and I had to really

step to catch up.

"You know how Maverick Cellars ended up with the property?"

"No."

"If Vic and Galbraith weren't getting along, why did Galbraith sell his farm to Maverick Cellars?"

"I said I don't know!" Matt headed around the truck on another lap and this time I let him go. I wasn't going to get anything more from him. I could see that. But if I had to wager on Matt, I'd say he knew perfectly well why and so therefore was lying. But why would he lie? If there wasn't so much work to do this morning, I would have put my mind on it, but right then I had to file it away for later and send Álvaro on his way.

Getting Galbraith's fruit crushed took the rest of the morning and we were still at it when lunch came around, which everybody skipped on account that most of us were going to Vic's funeral at one o'clock and wanted to finish everything before then. So that was why, after racing home to clean up and making a quick change and then picking up Jeff at his place since he also had to change for the funeral into his tie and jacket — for the second time in one week, which was for him a record — we finally arrived twenty minutes late to the cemetery, the outdoor service having already gotten started.

If I were the type of person who made top ten lists, and believe me when I say I'm not that kind of person, at the top of my list of all time favorite things to avoid would be going to funerals. It's right up there with going to the dentist. But just like going to the dentist you usually couldn't duck out of it. It wasn't the grieving or sadness, or the pain of loss you felt, or having to speak about the deceased in front of everybody if you got asked to do that, though that could certainly be painful all right, what made me want to avoid the whole mess was the crying. I just couldn't stand it. When the blubbering starts I would more than likely lose it and start crying right along with them, and I would give almost anything to avoid that. I could barely keep it in going to the movies, but at least then the theater was dark and afterward I could get it together before I went out again and people could see me. Of course, I've been known to tear up at an especially heartfelt car commercial on television.

Arriving at the cemetery, it caught me by surprise how many people had come, easily a couple of hundred, and it reminded me how popular Vic had been in the Valley. Everybody was already gathered around the spot where Vic's coffin would later be lowered into the ground. We had to search to find a place to park and barely found one amidst all the cars wedged in here and there and lining both sides of the graveled motorway that led into the cemetery. We headed on foot the rest of the way and pushed our way in closer.

Jeff was pulling at his collar. "I'm already hot. I'm loosening my tie."

I gave him a look, but he didn't stop until he had two buttons undone and the tie so loose it looked more like a muffler.

"Just take it off and put it in your pocket," I said. I knew the only way he would be completely comfortable was wearing flip-flops and a loin cloth, and that would definitely get more looks than if he showed up without his tie on.

He yanked it off in nothing flat and stuffed it into his pocket. "You don't want me passing out from heat exhaustion right in the middle of this thing."

"No, that would be embarrassing," I said. "C'mon."

At the center of the throng of mourners keeping the midday sun at bay was a tented awning over which the immediate family was seated and where the priest was in the middle of giving the eulogy. In front of them was Vic's coffin, draped in flowers with a large picture of him without his glasses and from the looks of it likely taken around ten years ago.

My eye was first drawn to the widow, Patricia, in the middle of the front row all in black and wearing a veil, holding tightly to the hand of her daughter, Frances, who was on her left side and doing her darnedest to manage a trembling lower lip. Sitting beside Frances was her husband Tom looking pale and somber and behind them in the next row were their three sad children. Next to Vic's grandchildren in the second row was Sheriff Coulette who was directly behind Patricia, his ears and face very red, needing perhaps to loosen his tie like Jeff had done, and filling out the remaining three rows were many of the relatives from out of town that had driven or flown in to be here, many of them I had met before and many I had not. On Patricia's right also in front was Vic's partner Benny with his elder sister Ruth who looked so old that I wondered for a moment how old Benny must be to have a sister that old. And last but not least, at the other end of the front row to Tom's left, my eyes having saved them for last for some reason, was Eric, glaring up at the priest who was reading an appropriate bible passage for the occasion, and sitting next to him with her hands in her lap was Rosalynd.

She was still with him and still looked good, better than good, and I would've thought more about how that made me feel if there hadn't been a sudden interruption that got me thinking about a whole mess of other things.

Patricia, who was facing the coffin and most of the other mourners that had come to pay their respects, and Jeff and I for that matter, not that anybody could see her face because of the veil anyway, had lifted her arm to point at somebody in the crowd. "She's not allowed here!"

I don't know if it was the sound of Patricia's dry voice or that she was wearing black, or if it was the rigid cast of her pointing arm, but I felt a cold shudder go through my body and roll through the crowd. The priest stopped his eulogy to gape at her along with nearly everybody else who wasn't try-ing to see where the hell Patricia was pointing.

"Make her leave!" she commanded, her arm still out-stretched and pointing. "She has no right to be here! Make her go!"

I was craning my neck over the crowd to see the person she was referring to, but there were just too many people moving around.

Then a female voice responded from the crowd, "I have just as much right to be here as anybody!"

"No you DON'T!"

"Yes, I do!" The voice quavered a bit at first, but held steady and then strengthened as it went along. "You're just afraid of what I might say! That these people might believe me!"

"Shut up!"

The crowd had stepped back from the voice to give her room and Jeff and I could finally see who the voice belonged to and she wasn't half bad. She was a few years older than me, and her make-up had smudged a bit around the eyes, which you made allowances for under the circumstances, but every-thing else was in top order.

"Vic would have wanted me here!"

"Tell her to shut up!" Patricia screeched.

"I won't shut up!"

But Patricia was now appealing to those around her. "I don't want her here! Someone make her leave!"

The Sheriff I saw was pinned in and couldn't make a move, but a couple of Patricia's male relatives got up from their seats to move the woman out and one even got a hand on her arm in short order. But the woman wasn't finished.

"You're afraid I'll tell them the truth!"

Patricia was still appealing, "Don't let her say these things."

The relatives got the woman firmly in hand and were making headway ushering her out, but she fought back and dropped her bomb.

"Murderer!" She got an arm free and pointed back at Patri-cia. "I know you killed him! You murdered Victor!"

A gasp went up from the crowd. The priest was now gaping at the woman instead of Patricia.

Patricia, of course, went right over the coffin after her. And that was the second time in a week I got to see Patricia's undergarments, which was twice too many times. She got about halfway over before tangling herself in the flower arrangement and knocking over Vic's ten year-old portrait, giving Tom and Eric enough time to catch up and get their hands on her.

The woman was still being ushered out, the crowd still in an uproar, and I elbowed Jeff who nodded and we followed after the woman. Beyond the bedlam of the crowd we could see the men releasing the woman and watched her go, now weeping toward her car. We proceeded across the grounds to head her off, but she got to her car in a hurry and started it up.

"Wait! I shouted. "We want to talk with you a minute!"

Her windows were rolled up and she had her car in gear and was rolling.

"Wait!"

As she drew abreast, she slowed down though she never came to a stop and cracked her window about an inch. I could see the tears running down her face and the mascara that was only smudged before was now a total wash.

"Who are you?" I said.

She said back defiantly, "Why don't you ask Patricia!" And then she gunned the tires, spitting gravel.

All Jeff and I could do was watch her go, or I thought that was all we could do.

"Don't sweat it," Jeff said. "I got her license plate number."

I glanced back impressed at his intrepidness and saw that we weren't the only ones who had followed the woman to her car. Standing next to us was Rosalynd.

As I registered that, Jeff went on, "If that's her car anyway. Easy enough to find out."

I looked again at the receding vehicle as it exited the cemetery, got onto the pavement and roared away. "Who the hell was that woman?"

"Well, isn't it obvious?" Rosalynd said. "She and Vic were having an affair."

Jeff and I both turned to her and at the same time exclaimed, "What?"

Chapter

10

KNOWING VIC AS well as I did you would think I would know if he was having an affair, or was even capable of having one. I mean, c'mon, how many office romances slip past without anybody even getting a glimmer? But I'll freely admit the idea had never crossed my mind, and now that Rosalynd had pointed it out to us, of course it was obvious. Maybe women are more sensitive to that kind of thing, or maybe they just pay more attention to it. Or maybe it was just guys don't wonder why other guys are in a good mood. A silly grin in the morning or an added spring in Vic's stride as he left work some evening headed for his secret rendezvous with romance I more than likely would've chalked up to the Giants' recent sweep of the Dodgers in a doubleheader, so I just stood there and stared, marveling at her insight.

Rosalynd, watching us, had that smile of hers going.

Jeff eyes were twinkling. "Never suspected Vic could be so frisky!"

"Me neither," I said. "The old dog!"

Rosalynd giggled, and I smiled back at her.

"Well," Jeff said, "we wanted a clear motive."

I nodded.

"Marital infidelity's a clear motive."

"Yep," I said.

So all three of us turned our attention toward the clear motive still on display behind us.

Patricia, still fuming, could be glimpsed amongst the voluble crowd, seated once more under the tented awning and being consoled by her two children Eric and Frances. Benny and Tom were at the casket refitting the flowers and repositioning Vic's portrait under the harried guidance of the priest, while fending off the fallout as best he could was Sheriff Coulette. That woman's outburst had put him in an awkward position, both political and familial, and he was not a happy camper. I could see that from here. I then saw him focus his gaze in our direction while many others near him also craned their necks to give us a gander and for a moment our eyes met. No, he was definitely not happy.

"Maybe somebody will tell us who she is," Rosalynd said.

"Maybe that's what Eric's coming over for," Jeff said.

Eric had noticed the Sheriff and the others looking and had looked over this way himself and had noticed us. He was now pushing through the crowd, having abruptly broken it off with his mother, and we watched him come.

The way his body was leaning into it, I decided I'd better get the first poke in, verbal or otherwise, before he actually got to us or prepare to be steamrolled. So I said, "Hey, Eric, any idea who that woman was?"

"Chris, Goddamnit!" His eyes were glaring and his jaw was jutting, but he kept coming and didn't say anything more until he reached us and had squared up his feet. "Why can't you keep your nose out of other people's business?"

"What business is that?"

"You know perfectly well what business! I've had it up to here—" and he gestured past his forehead so we would all know how far he'd had had it, "—with you and all your bullshit! Going around, trying to make everybody think you're the only one who cared about Vic. Well, you're not! He was my father, not yours! Why can't you get that through your thick head?"

The topic at hand if you could call it that had suddenly taken an altogether different turn. We were no longer discussing what that woman had blurted out, but something much more personal – me!

"Eric, time out," I said. "You could be right about my thick head, I'll give you that, but you're wrong if you think I ever wanted to get between you and your father."

"Spare me your bullshit! I don't want to hear it!" He turned abruptly to go, trying to win another argument by leaving and snapped heatedly at Rosalynd. "C'mon!"

I saw her spine straighten at his tone.

"I said, c'mon, Goddamnit! What're you waiting for, a gilded invitation?"

But she didn't move. She didn't even respond to his demand. Instead, she turned to me and calmly asked, "Will you take me home?"

I had just got though telling Eric that he was wrong if he thought I ever wanted to get between him and his father, and now almost immediately his girlfriend was asking me to do just that and get between her and him. The only difference was that this time I wanted to. From the look on Eric's face, the difference wasn't lost on him either. Already flushed with emotion, he was boiling up to an even deeper shade of red, and there was no telling what he'd do next. Added to that, it was no secret Eric fully expected to inherit his father's interest in Maverick Cellars, and if he had any say in the matter, and from everything I knew or suspected of him he had plenty of say, he would more than likely end up being my boss. Rosalynd was asking me in a sense to choose her welfare over my job security, and of course the choice was easy.

"Sure, I'll take you home."

Eric made a noise like his wind was being punched out. Then his neck bowed and all at once he started toward Rosalynd, reaching for her arm, so I stepped in between and blocked it.

Eric came up, his eyes glaring hotly at me. "Keep standing in my way, Chris, and just see what happens!"

"You need to cool off," I said.

"Just keep it up!" And he gave me a stiff shove. I kept my

feet and thought Eric was going to follow it up with something stronger, and so did he, except he made a quick glance behind me and to my right and that got him thinking better of it.

The only thing behind me and to my right was Jeff.

He turned his glare back on me. "We'll finish this! Don't think we won't! Next time, your enforcer won't be around!"

Without looking back, Eric spun and marched off, and I let him win the argument this time and turned to Rosalynd.

"You okay?"

She nodded, "Yes, thank you. I'm okay."

Behind me, Jeff was still watching Eric go. When his eyes returned to us, he saw the questioning look on my face and said, "I didn't do anything! I thought you were handling things just fine."

"So did I," Rosalynd said.

I nodded at her and shrugged modestly, 'what the heck'? I figured I'd make it unanimous.

Eric's threats had no longer made us feel very welcome, and so we decided to skip what was left of the service and do as Rosalynd had asked and take her home. Apparently, home for her didn't mean we had to drive all the way back to San Francisco, but only to a modest house in Stag's Leap, the owners of which were family friends who happened to be out of the country this month, and so Rosalynd had the run of the place.

Rosalynd sat between us on the bench seat of my truck as we headed down valley on the Silverado Trail. She was looking out the window at the vineyards passing by and seemed to be enjoying herself. I was too, to be honest, with her hip pressed lightly up against mine on the bench seat and the smell of her so close. She certainly was pretty, I had to remind myself to stop glancing at her and keep my eyes on the road ahead.

"Having fun?" I asked her.

"Oh, I've never ridden in a pickup truck before," she said, grinning that grin of hers.

"No kidding?"

"No. It's a new experience for me. It feels — very rugged. Sitting here, I feel ready for anything!"

I shared a glance with Jeff who was pressed up against her other hip. His look was incredulous, 'Never ridden in a pickup before?' But I didn't think that was entirely fair. I suspected Rosalynd was only sharing a part of herself with us and I took it as a compliment.

But there was something more on my mind, and Jeff's, I was sure, that we needed to learn from Rosalynd and we kind of had her trapped between us, so I went ahead and asked, "Ready, say, to talk about Eric?"

"And what just happened?" she added.

"Yep."

She didn't say anything for a moment. Then she said, "I think you already know most of it."

"Probably."

"I don't," Jeff said.

Rosalynd was still turned toward me. "But you'd like me to fill in the parts you may not already know."

"Yep."

"Like everything," Jeff went on.

"Like if I think Eric had motive enough to kill his father."

"Like that," Jeff conceded.

"Do you?" I asked.

"Yes and no."

Jeff snorted at that answer, but all Rosalynd did was smile at him before going on.

"I know he's in financial trouble. He didn't come right out and tell me that, but I got that impression, and also I found out a few things."

"Not that you were being nosey."

"Certainly not. Like for instance, I know Eric approached his father for a substantial loan. You know about his restaurant?"

I nodded.

"Well, he doesn't want anybody to know, but it's about to go under."

"And Vic, what? Turned him down?"

"Yes, he refused. Something about not throwing good money after bad."

I nodded.

"Then I learned," Rosalynd waved her hand, "no matter how, that Eric had asked if his father would talk to Gerry Zacks for him about the loan, and Vic said absolutely not. He was so adamant about it, he even forbade Eric from approaching Zacks on his own."

"That's very interesting," I said.

"Yeah, interesting," Jeff echoed. "What's up with Gerry Zacks?"

"I don't know," I said. "But his name keeps popping up."

"Popping up, how?" Rosalynd asked.

"No matter how far afield we get," I said, "Gerry Zacks seems to have some sort of connection."

"As far as we know," Jeff corrected. "Zacks hasn't exactly been around much lately to find out one way or another how connected he actually is."

"Won't even answer his phone," I added.

"Chris has tried."

Rosalynd nodded at us.

I said to her, "Did you get asked to make a donation to the 'Save Eric's Restaurant Fund?'"

"Well,' Rosalynd said, "he hinted around about it, but no. He never made me a concrete proposal."

"Proposal, huh?" I said, an eyebrow going up.

I saw her eyes flash at me for an instant and that hint of amusement in them. "But now, with what has happened, I doubt if he'll make me one."

"A proposal?"

"Yes."

"On account of Chris standing in his way," Jeff said.

"On account of that, and that he'll never get anything from me anyway."

"So he's desperate for money," I said.

"I'd say that's a clear motive," Jeff said.

"So would I," I agreed.

"The bastard," he growled. "I knew Eric belonged at the top of our list—"

"But you haven't yet heard the no part," interrupted Rosalynd.

"Which is?" Jeff asked.

"I don't think he did it." Off of our dubious looks she went on, "I've been seeing him lately, which of course you already know, and I don't think he has that kind of passion in him."

"I don't know," Jeff said. "He seemed passionate enough to threaten Chris on account of you!"

She just shrugged. "Well, that's different."

As we approached the turnoff that led to where she was staying, Rosalynd pointed it out to us and I turned in. The private road first spanned a dry culvert, then led between cabernet sauvignon vineyards that lined each side up to a fieldstone entry with an electronic gate that Rosalynd opened with a remote she had in her purse. The road continued on around a bend a short ways before we finally caught sight of the house, or more precisely chateau, having been hidden from view by the landscape, an eighteenth century style straight out of the Loire Valley from the looks of it with more rooms than centuries. If this was what Rosalynd thought of as modest, I was thinking, how the hell much money did her family actually have? The grounds in front were graveled, and off to one side, I saw Rosalynd's convertible parked under a portico so I headed for it.

I stopped the truck next to hers and we hopped out.

"You're positive," I asked, "you want us to just leave you

out here?"

"If you're worried about Eric showing up after you go, don't. I'll be driving back to the City."

"Oh," I said. "All right."

Then Rosalynd thanked both of us for our gallantry and gave Jeff a hug, and then turned to me and gave me a hug too. The top of her head came just to the bridge of my nose, and I caught the subtle perfume of her again before she broke it off. She stood close and looked me in the eye for a moment, and I looked back and saw the amusement dancing and then she took out a piece of paper from her purse and handed it to me.

"My cell phone. If you want to chat sometime."

"I still owe you that croissant," I said, putting the paper in my wallet.

"I'm looking forward to it."

Jeff and I got back in my truck and we followed the drive around, and as we came about we waved good-bye to Rosalynd and headed out. Just before we rounded the bend leaving the house behind, I glanced back in my rearview mirror and saw her still standing there, watching us go.

I looked over at Jeff and saw that he was watching me closely. "What?" I said.

Jeff kept eyeing me.

"Don't tell me this time you didn't find her helpful."

Jeff made a face and grunted. "She could still be a double agent."

Chapter

11

I DROVE JEFF back to his place, and while we were headed there, we talked about Patricia and Eric and whether or not their respective motives were sufficient enough to move the Sheriff to investigate further. The answer was obviously, no. First, Patricia and Eric were family and that hurdle was still too high; and second, he probably already knew more about it than we did at the present, or if he didn't know more, he probably didn't want to hear anymore about it. We needed something more substantial than unfounded accusations hurled over coffins to get him to move. We needed proof.

Jeff had left his squad car in his driveway, planning to head back to work right after the funeral, and that was where we headed once I got my truck edged in off the street. We climbed into the front seat and Jeff got out the license plate number he had written down off that woman's car and punched it into his dashboard computer. In moments we had her name and home address.

"Bridget Monroe," Jeff read off the screen.

"You gotta be kidding me," I said. "That can't be her real name."

"It's what's on her driver's license."

"Then she changed it."

"Oh, I don't know. It kind of fits, if you think about it."

I took a moment and did and had to concede he might be right. Bridget Monroe.

"We can head over there right now," Jeff offered. "If you want to."

"I thought you had to clock in."

"I've got some vacation time."

But I had been thinking on that before we had looked her up, so instead I said, "How willing do you think she'd be answering questions from the both of us?"

Jeff thought about it. "Might be intimidating."

"That's what I was thinking. And you're an officer of the law."

He was nodding, "Yeah, she might not want to open up if I was there." I could hear the disappointment in his voice.

"She might open up if I came alone. She probably already knows who I am from Vic."

"Yeah, you're probably right."

So that was how it turned out, me heading over to Ms.

Monroe's place and Jeff heading back to work, but not before he had me go over some of the questions I was going to ask and had offered his advice. We agreed to meet up later at the Wine Rustler, a restaurant and bar in downtown Napa, which the Sheriff's Department was currently favoring as a hangout.

Ms. Monroe's address was in the hills east of Napa where it remained mostly rural with more pastures for livestock and horses than planted vineyards, though that was more and more of a rarity these days. I found her number handwritten on the mailbox at the roadside and pulled into her gravel driveway that skirted the immediate neighbor on the right. I gleaned from the sign next to Ms. Monroe's mailbox that her immediate neighbor was an award-winning breeder of cutting horses. I also might've gotten that idea on my own without the sign on account of all the horses and stables and trailers and arenas and pastures and more horses all over the place. The smell alone might've tipped me off. Breeding cutting horses was apparently good business. Now if I only knew what the heck a cutting horse was.

I recognized her car parked in front of her place with relief, both for finding the right house and finding her hopefully home. The house was a modest ranch style with an emphasis on modest, not Rosalynd's kind of modest, either. What lawn there was in front had gone to seed long ago and had been allowed to dry up, and from where Ms. Monroe had put her car, was now used mostly as parking space. The house was facing the stables across the graveled drive, and I pulled in next to her car, killed the engine and got out.

A horse whinnied. There was a large picture window next to the entry, but the angle of the sun made it impossible to see through, reflecting everything back like a mirror. I headed past it to the front door, running my hands through my hair in the glass and straightening my tie before knocking.

In a moment, the door opened and standing there was Bridget Monroe. She had washed her face since I had seen her last, no more mascara running, and had changed into different clothes. She now wore a loose-fitting diaphanous garment obviously designed for lounging comfortably around the house or better, the boudoir, and I might add, did little to cover up her many assets. Up close, she looked younger than I had first thought she was. Evidently she had recovered some from the emotional turmoil at the cemetery, though not completely. Her eyes looked out warily at me and she waited for me to speak. A horse whinnied again.

"Ms. Monroe?"

"Yes," she answered, her eyes flashing. "I see you found out my name. Did you ask Patricia?"

"Actually, no," I said. "The last I saw of her, she was in no mood to answer any questions."

"I bet!" she spat. Then she regarded me for a moment. "So what do you want?"

"We've never met," I started.

"I know who you are. You're Vic's protégé."

I nodded, "Chris Garrett," and held out my hand, smiling.

Ms. Monroe hesitated for a moment and I thought she might close the door on me, but instead took my offered hand just as that horse whinnied again, this time much closer, and both of us turned to look. A beautiful stallion, shiny black with white speckles on its rump was rearing up on its hind legs. Some of Ms. Monroe's neighbors were holding on expertly with a lead rope. The horse was showing a great amount of spirit.

Ms. Monroe clung to my hand for a moment as we watched, and I noticed how soft her skin was.

"I suppose you want to ask me some questions," she said.

"That was the idea."

She finally let go of my hand. "C'mon, inside." She let the door swing wide and I followed her in. That gown she was wearing certainly didn't leave much to the imagination.

We could still hear the stallion whinnying even with the front door shut, and the large picture window framing the view outside of pastures and horses also gave us a clear view of the rearing stallion.

"This is quite a view you've got," I said.

"That stallion's Quiet Dancer, though there's nothing quiet about him right now! He's the number one ranked cutting horse in the nation. Grand National Champion or something, I forget."

"I was meaning to ask, what's a cutting horse?"

"Ever been to the rodeo?"

"Sure."

"Ever watch 'em use horses to remove a steer from a

cattle herd?"

I nodded.

"That's called cutting. Cutting from the herd. Quiet Dancer is the very best at it."

The stallion was still up on his hind legs whinnying, and I realized why. In a small arena nearby they had a ready mare on lead, and they were bringing the stallion to her. That whinnying was a frustrated scream of sexual tension. I wasn't sure, but it seemed hotter inside the house.

"Umm, Ms. Monroe—" I said, trying to remember the questions Jeff had wanted me to ask, "I wanted to ask you why, umm—"

"Why I said what I did at the funeral?"

"Yeah."

The stallion was now whinnying nonstop as they drew him into the arena, and still rearing. The breeders were having trouble keeping a tight hold on him.

"Have you any proof?" I asked.

"That Patricia murdered Vic?" Her eyes flashed again. "Hell, yeah! She shot at us! With a gun!"

"Why, for God's sakes?"

For a second I thought Ms. Monroe might dodge, but then her lips upturned playfully at me.

"She caught you and Vic together, didn't she?" I asked.

She nodded and giggled. "She sure did! Caught us making love in bed!" When she giggled her body made that diaphanous fabric do marvelous things.

"And she pulled a gun on you." My voice was drying up

on me.

Ms. Monroe had her hand on my sleeve.

"And shot at us! Luckily, she missed."

Outside, the neighbors had the mare turned toward the stallion and had rubbed on some sort of lubricant to help the process along.

I swallowed, trying not to look, but it did little good. I asked hoarsely, "Did you call the police?"

Ms. Monroe was watching what was happening outside as well. "First we ran!" she said. "Then Vic called the Sheriff's Office. But in the end, he wouldn't press charges."

The progress outside with the stallion and mare had transfixed both of us. I couldn't turn away, and apparently neither could Ms. Monroe. I felt her hand tighten on my arm. The stallion, screaming like mad, was finally given rein and reared up onto the mare, but on the first try missed and was brought down again. The next time was on target, and I swear to God that horse looked three stories tall. The massive muscles of his body began to heave and thrust, the whinnying replaced by thick throaty grunting.

I heard a moan escape Ms. Monroe. When I looked at her, her eyes locked on mine and with only a shrug of her shoulders that diaphanous fabric of hers fell to the floor. She had nothing on underneath. Only women wear clothes that can be removed so effortlessly I was thinking, and then she was pressing her body against mine, her arms wrapped around me, her lips seeking mine.

Blood had filled my head so thickly I couldn't think

straight any longer, but I managed somehow to push her away. I had to get out of there. Right now! I staggered drunkenly toward the door, and out. Ms. Monroe followed me to the door apparently not embarrassed at all that the neighbors might see her. I made it to my truck and somehow got it in gear and got the hell out of there, and it took all I had not to run off into a ditch. It was fifteen minutes before I was breathing regularly again.

"So, there you have it," I said later to Jeff wrapping up what had happened, having confessed everything. "As you can see, Vic was doomed." Jeff was sitting next to me at the bar. We had met up at the Wine Rustler after he had gotten off work. I had come straight from Maverick Cellars, where everything was ship shape, and now it was almost seven. Jeff was so entertained by my play-by-play of events out at Ms. Monroe's place that tears of hilarity were flowing down his cheeks. He couldn't even drink his beer from all the cackling he was doing. He managed to squeak out, "C'mere, big fella. Show me whatcha got!"

"Go ahead and laugh. You weren't there."

"God, I wish I had!"

"Oh, no you don't." I said. "That would've made it even worse," which set him off cackling again.

Jeff had to grip the edge of the bar to keep his seat. When he finally got control of himself, he said, "She's definitely got the jones for winemakers. First Vic, then you! Her name oughta be Bridget Bordeaux!"

"Very funny."

For the next half hour or so, Jeff couldn't look straight at me without repressing a grin.

I asked him, "So, you want another beer?"

"I haven't finished my first one," and he took a sip, which seemed to settle him some.

"You have to admit, we did learn something," I said. "I believe firing a weapon at another person in anger is against the law."

"Yeah," he admitted. "It is."

"So why isn't Patricia up to her eyelashes in trouble?"

"That's a good question. Actually, that's why I asked you down here. I've been poking around on my end and uncovered some dirt, and the pal who helped uncover it will be here any minute."

"Yeah?" I asked, looking around.

"He's a little late, but he'll show."

"Oh."

So we sat back and drank our beers.

"Want something to eat?" I picked up one of the menus on the bar.

Jeff shrugged. "What do they got?"

"Mostly appetizers. Here's one that sounds good, Goat Cheese with Duck Rillette."

Jeff made a face. "Goat cheese?"

"What's wrong with that? You like cheese."

"Yeah, but I hate goats!"

"What's wrong with goats?"

"I hate 'em. I don't like how they smell. They're smelly animals."

I laughed.

He went on, "Remember the Prices from high school? Peggy Price?"

I nodded.

"They had goats," as if that explained it.

"I don't remember that."

"You have to. They had 'em in their house!"

"They had goats in their house?" I asked incredulously.

"Yeah, don't you remember? They were always butting into you all the time."

I wasn't recalling any goats in Peggy Price's house.

Jeff tried to help, "Remember, the Prices had that health food store."

"The Prices had a health food store?"

"That's why they had the goats! They sold the milk!"

I shook my head. With all that had been going on lately, my memory was nearly shot. "I must be getting middle-aged Alzheimer's," I said, feeling suddenly exhausted. "I can't remember any of this."

"You remember Peggy's father flew helicopters, don't you? For the hospital?"

"Well, yeah."

"See? There's nothing wrong with your memory." And he waved at the bartender, having finally finished his beer and needing a refill.

So we skipped the goat cheese, but the duck rillette wasn't bad, spread on some toasted baguette pieces. They also brought cornichons to go with it, but the pickles didn't go as well with the beer.

Not too much longer Jeff's pal showed. When he came through the door, Jeff waved him over and said to me, "Chris, Deputy Murray."

I held out my hand as Jeff told him who I was, but Deputy Murray shied away.

"You're that guy blabbed to the paper!" he accused me.

"Hold on," Jeff said. "Chris had nothing to do with that!"

Murray wasn't buying.

I let my unshaken hand fall.

Jeff went on, "He was bushwhacked!"

"That's true," I said.

But the deputy was still shy. He said furtively, "Yeah, well, all I know is, things that happen around this guy get in the paper! I don't want my name in the paper!"

"They won't," Jeff said. A booth had emptied, and Jeff grabbed Murray before he could escape and steered him toward it for more privacy. "How 'bout a beer? Chris is buying."

I nodded encouragingly.

Murray finally consented and slid into the booth with Jeff and told me what he wanted, so I headed back to the bar to get Murray his drink. When I got back, Murray had switched places with Jeff, taking the gunfighter's position with his back to the wall. He could see the whole place from that seat and seemed a little less anxious. I slid in next to Jeff and handed Murray his drink. He glanced at it, but his eyes were more interested in me. I met his gaze and tried to look trustworthy.

"Beckwell says you're all right, so I guess you are." He took a small sip of his beer, and went on, "What I'm gonna tell you goes no place else, understand?"

"Absolutely."

He looked around the joint first before saying more, seemed satisfied and took a bigger sip of his beer. "I was told to forget this happened, and I have. Until this moment. After I tell you, I'm forgetting for good, so don't expect me to back you up!"

"Gotcha," I said.

Jeff said, "Tell us."

"Me and Pontoriero got the call — a domestic disturbance between Victor Miranda and his wife, Patricia. Seems she fired a pistol at him and some chick Vic was fooling around with."

"Yeah," Jeff was nodding.

"We know about that," I said.

"The hell you do!" Murray said in disbelief.

"The chick, she bared all to Chris," Jeff explained, and couldn't keep his face straight and a laugh escaped.

I shot him a look.

"Sorry," he said to me.

Murray was looking back and forth between us, missing the joke. "If you already know—"

Jeff prompted, "Go ahead. Tell us what happened next."

"We caught up with Vic's wife. Pulled her over in her Lexus and she still had the weapon, an S&W .38 if you want to know, belonging to her husband. She didn't want to cooperate and for a second it looked dicey, but she finally tossed the weapon out and we took her into custody."

"You had guns drawn on her?" Jeff asked.

He nodded. "Hammers back and everything. We weren't fooling around."

"Why was all this hushed up?" I asked.

"Vic wouldn't press charges, and hell, Patricia's the Sheriff's sister for Chrissake! The publicity alone would've been embarrassing for everybody."

Jeff asked, "What do you think, now that Vic has had his unfortunate accident?"

"I don't think!" He was getting anxious again. "As a matter of fact, as of right now I'm forgetting what the hell we're talking about!" He chugged down the rest of his beer and got up. "Thanks for the brew. I won't be seeing you!" And split.

I slid around to the other side of the booth and faced Jeff. Now that we knew what we knew, what were we going to do with it? I kept my voice down, though I had little concern of being overheard with the noise in the place, "I'm beginning to understand why the Sheriff hasn't been all that excited to call Vic's death anything but an accident."

Jeff kept his voice lowered too. "Not when his sister's got the clearest motive."

"Yeah, one he had a hand in keeping off the books."

I watched Jeff wrestle with this new information.

"It still might not mean anything," he said. "I mean if word of this got out, the Sheriff's reelection campaign would be in a hell of a panic."

"Not to mention the black eye it would give Maverick Cellars."

He nodded. "But Patricia still might not've done it."

"In your professional opinion, could she physically have done it?"

"Pushed Vic in?" He thought about it. "If she caught him offguard, sure."

I didn't say anything.

Jeff saw that something was bothering me. "What is it?"

"Patricia," I said. "If she wanted to kill him, why would she wait to push him into that vat? She had him dead to rights in bed with Ms. Monroe. She could've plugged him then."

"But she missed."

"Yeah."

He nodded, catching on. "Maybe the gunshot was only a warning."

"To stop the fooling around."

"Un-huh. But he didn't take the warning."

"So later, she finished the job."

Jeff's shoulders went up. "Could've happened that way."

I nodded, but I still wasn't sure. Before we could continue, a female voice called above the hubbub, "Chris Garrett!"

I looked up and it was Jennifer Kimura. For a split second I thought she might've overheard us talking even with the noise.

But then I realized she was too far away, unless she was a lip-reader. She made a beeline for us, taking the shortest route through the tables filled with other restaurant patrons.

"How are you?" she asked as she arrived, and then before I could respond, bent across the table to get a good look at Jeff's face. "And this must be your friend, Officer—"

"Deputy Beckwell, ma'am."

She had her tiny hand out, and Jeff being a gentleman accepted it, and she used it as an excuse to slide in next to him. He gave me a look that said, 'what do I do?' and when he saw I had no help to offer whatsoever, he made room for her. What else could he do?

Jennifer was all smiles. From past experience I had reason to be leery of that smile, cute as it was, and my guard was up.

"Heard there was a little drama at the funeral this afternoon!" she said, her eyes big and sparkly. "I oughta follow you two around just to stay abreast of the action!" She nuzzled in closer to Jeff and said, "Heard you were right in the middle of it!"

"Hello, Jennifer." I finally got in. Then I said, "You heard wrong."

She looked at me suspiciously.

"Besides," I said, "I'm not sure I want to talk to you. Not after what happened the last time."

"Whatever are you saying?"

"Somebody leaked that stuff about me to the paper."

She was shocked, or rather making a good show of being

shocked. "How could you think that of me?" She grasped Jeff's arm in appeal. "How could he?"

"Because you're really good at what you do," I said. She started to make her denial, but I cut her off. "Now, don't try to dodge. Who else had the connections to get that story to the paper?"

She was all set to stay with the dodge, but she saw I wasn't buying any of it, so instead she smiled sweetly and shrugged. "Okay, you caught me."

Jeff blurted, "So it was you called the Sentinel?"

"I just admitted it, didn't I?" Then she appealed to me, "I thought it was what you wanted, Chris."

"What I wanted," I repeated.

"I was trying to help."

"Yeah," Jeff growled. "Help paint a target on Chris' back!"

"Oh, you think Chris might be in danger?" Jennifer was now at Jeff, biting her lower lip with concern.

"C'mon," I said to Jeff getting out of the booth. "We gotta go, Jennifer."

Jennifer made a lunge and grabbed my hand to keep me in place. "You're being so difficult! Did somebody threaten you? Is that it?"

"Jennifer," I said, twisting my wrist to get my hand free, but keeping my voice upbeat. "It was just fabulous! We'll have to do this again sometime!"

"Chris—" she was going for my hand again.

But I was too fast for her. I looked over at Jeff. He was

still trapped.

Jennifer turned to him. "You'll make him sit back down, won't you? Let's all have a drink!"

Jeff said, "Uh, no" and started pushing her out of the booth. He had eighty pounds on her, so it was no contest.

"Well," she declared, righting herself as Jeff clambered out. Then she turned her big eyes on me. "Don't be mad. I would feel miserable if you were mad." She had that lower lip of hers pushed out.

"I'm not mad," I said. "And I doubt you'd feel much of anything if I was."

"Not true!"

I let that go.

"You promise, you're not mad?"

"I'll go farther than that," I said. "I'll admit I'm not even mad you leaked that bit about me to the paper. Just don't do it again."

"Alright," she said, the smile sneaking back. "I promise." She even put her hand across her heart.

"Okay," I said and smiled too.

She wanted a hug, so I gave her one, though I wasn't convinced she was being completely honest. Jeff got a hug too, though he had just met her, and she tried once more to get us to stay and gossip, but we were having none of that. Luckily, a smartly dressed couple happened in just then that Jennifer recognized and thought important enough not to ignore, and we didn't, and she was momentarily distracted. It was all the advantage we needed to make our escape. And we did.

Chapter 12

PATRICIA'S RUN IN with the law wasn't the only thing Jeff and I discussed after leaving the restaurant. Before heading home, we stood awhile in the parking lot near my truck and I brought him up to date on Matt Bakerwood and what Matt had said earlier and what he hadn't said about the vintner Galbraith. I gave Jeff the whole crop – how Maverick Cellars along with Zacks' help had acquired Galbraith's property though I still didn't know the particulars, and how Vic and Galbraith hadn't seen eye to eye, and what Tony had told me and everything else I knew. Jeff agreed with me that it was worth following up, especially if Galbraith held any deeper animosity toward Vic than what had been hinted at. Patricia's guilt wasn't entirely sewed up to our satisfaction anyway.

So when both of us started trading more yawns back and forth than opinions and with the sun already down, we decided to call it a day. Jeff said he would call me tomorrow and maybe we could meet up around lunch, and I thought that was a good idea and we each headed home. As I drove I let recent events wash over me so completely that I was already parked in my spot at Marjorie's and killing the engine and headlights before I realized I had arrived.

I was still hungry so when I got into my apartment I dug into the fridge and found some leftover Chinese from the night before and nuked it in the microwave. Princess Woo's Seven Secrets wasn't exactly what I desired, but it was edible. I thought about turning on the T.V., but with every channel delivering nothing but hyped-up excitement in a vain attempt to keep a channel-switching audiences' full attention, I decided to skip it. Instead I set my alarm clock and dropped my clothes where I peeled them off and climbed into bed, and dreamed all night about screaming horses, fermenting wine and drowning.

—∞—

I had the sneaking suspicion the next day wasn't going to be much better than my restless night had been when first off, as I pulled into Maverick Cellars that morning around six-thirty, I saw Eric's Black X5 Beemer parked in my spot.

Initially, the game plan today was to finish crushing the fruit from Galbraith's old place like we had done the day before at both Maverick Cellars and Bakerwood Winery simultaneously. Álvaro and our team would tackle the grapes sent to

Maverick Cellars, while I would pick up the ball with Matt's crew over at Bakerwood Winery. And in a way we were still planning to do that, crushing at both places, except since yesterday a new wrinkle had developed. When I had my truck parked in another space and had headed into the winery, Benny who was also here early this morning had quickly pulled me aside and told me of Eric's intention to run the crew today at Maverick Cellars.

Eric wanted to take on more responsibility around the place since his father's death, and how under those circumstances could Benny say 'no' to him? He hoped I understood, and I nodded, knowing full well what this move of Eric's meant. Eric, out on the crush pad, had noticed me when I first walked in, but now apparently was so busy setting up for the arrival of Tony's fruit that he didn't have time to even point out how dumb I was.

Looking back at Benny, he had never look so used up to me — like he had aged fifteen years in the past couple of days, or maybe he was just getting the kind of sleep I was currently getting — so I decided to be Zen about it, knowing Álvaro would be there to keep an eye on Eric, and I would unobtrusively as possible go back and forth between the two wineries and coordinate. That should work out all right, I told Benny, as long as Eric didn't start countermanding my winemaking decisions, and Benny assured me he wouldn't. He hadn't brought up the incident I had had with Eric yesterday at the funeral, like he hadn't brought up the tiff with the Mirandas at the wine dinner though both of us had it clearly in mind as we discussed this new arrangement. A storm was brewing on the horizon, and neither of us wanted to dwell on it right then. When Álvaro arrived, I filled him in on the change of plans and he took it with a shrug and a laugh, which was one of the reasons we got on so well. But before hopping to it, Benny had one more thing he needed to tell me. Apparently Patricia had asked him to tell me she wanted to speak with me this morning and had summoned me to do so at the house. I was to stop by on my way to Bakerwood Winery. She hadn't specified exactly what she wanted to speak to me about, but I already had a pretty good guess.

Vic and Patricia's place was only a short ways north of the winery, and was sort of an updated farmhouse, meaning that it had once been a farmhouse but had been recently renovated to impress even the Rothschilds if they happened to visit – and they very well might have, come to think of it. Surrounding the house were grape vineyards on all sides, and as I drove my truck up the drive what commanded attention first was the large ceramic fountain in front. The driveway circled the fountain and I stopped my truck at the entry. Off to the right under a breezeway that connected the house with the automobile salon – I'm not kidding, Patricia once referred to it that way – was parked her late model Lexus and Vic's SUV. Perfectly normal, I noted, seeing Vic's vehicle parked there, but I stared at it for a moment. Somebody must've moved it from Maverick Cellars to here, and why not? But still I stared.

I rang the doorbell and after a moment the door opened and I saw Frances looking out at me.

"Hello, Chris," she said in an underwhelming voice and didn't smile at me like she usually does, but she did open the door wide.

As I stepped inside, I said, "Morning, Frances," but she had already shut the door and had turned her back on me.

She headed across the foyer and said without turning, "I'm glad you didn't say, 'good morning' because it certainly isn't. I don't expect to see a good morning for quite some time."

I was still rooted at the entry, and Frances finally noticing this, turned and feigning patience beckoned, "C'mon. Follow me, if you're here to see Mother."

Frances led me through some French doors and out onto the veranda that ran the full length of the back of the house. The whole of the Napa Valley seemed to spread out between the pillars holding up the roof, and sitting outside at a tile-covered table having her breakfast was Patricia.

She looked as tired as Benny had to me. Her shoulders sagged, her whole body sagged and she was frowning. When I stepped up to the table with Frances, Patricia turned the frown on me and demanded, "Why are you still stirring up trouble?"

"Mother!" Frances exclaimed. "I thought we decided you weren't going to talk like that."

Patricia did an abrupt turnaround. "You're right, you're right. I'm sorry." And she waved it away. "I don't know why I started— I never intended—" Then she was waving me over, "Chris, you come and sit down. Don't mind me, I'm just being hysterical, that's all."

Frances was still eyeing her, but seemed satisfied her mother wasn't going to go off again.

I did as Patricia asked and took a chair at the tile-covered table. She had lifted an insulated carafe and was pouring me a cup of coffee.

"You'll have some coffee?"

"Sure," I said, going along since she had already poured it. No sense wasting it. I sat down and took up the cream, put some in and then had at the sugar.

"You're probably wondering why I asked you to stop by."

"I can probably guess," I said.

Patricia attempted to smile. "I'm sure you can."

Then she turned to her daughter and said, "Frances dear, you don't mind leaving us for a bit? That's a good girl."

For a second I thought Frances was going to protest, and so did she, but instead she just nodded at her mother and with a short glance at me strolled back inside.

Patricia was rubbing at her temples. "The last couple of days have been very difficult. I'm sure you can well imagine. The house has been completely full of people and relatives and all sorts, since – well, you know how long."

I did.

"This is the first moment I've had to myself, and – well, as you can see I have this terrific headache."

I could see, especially how pinched it made her face look.

Patricia had been working on a banana before I had stepped onto the veranda to join her, adding it to a bowl of granola, and she went back to the fruit and finished cutting it into bites. Then without hesitating, she lifted the peel and slapped it across her forehead.

I might have gawked.

Tilting her head so the banana skin didn't slide off she got her eyes back on me and went on, "Did you go see that woman?"

"Uh, yes I did," I said.

"I thought you would. What, you go out to her house, next to that horse breeder?"

I nodded, and the memory made it hard to keep looking Patricia in the eye, so I got suddenly interested in my cup of coffee. I took a sip. Not bad.

"It's no wonder that woman's oversexed," she said with a great deal of disdain. "Did she tell you what happened?"

"She told me you shot at them with a gun."

Patricia adjusted the banana skin, and then waved that away. "I wasn't trying to kill them. I just wanted to scare them a little."

"Were they scared?"

"You better believe it!" And then she laughed, though her eyes didn't look all that amused. "They ran outside! Knocked the screen right off the slider getting out! Both of them with no clothes on!"

I took another sip of coffee.

"You probably think I'm crazy," she said.

"No, I don't," I assured her, though I had to force myself not to glance up at the banana peel.

"Well, I'm not. And I wanted to tell you that I didn't kill my husband. I never wanted to kill him that night with the gun. I just wanted him to stop fooling around with that woman."

"Did he stop?"

"I don't know. I think he might have."

I nodded.

"Do you know why I wanted to tell you?"

"I think I do," I said.

"Because I know how you felt about Vic, how much you cared about him, and I know how hard it's been for you to accept his death as an accident. I thought, if you knew what happened, you wouldn't spread any more gossip about me."

I didn't think it would do any good to explain that I hadn't spread any gossip in the first place. So I just nodded again.

"Do you believe I never wanted to kill my husband?"

"I think I do."

"You do?"

"Yes," I said, and I was telling her the truth, unless I was shown evidence of something stronger, like say a candid photo of her hoisting Vic by his belt over the catwalk railing and into that vat.

"You won't tell anybody about this?"

"I won't," I promised.

Patricia took the banana peel off her forehead, and her frown had gone away. She softly asked, "Do you still think someone killed my husband?"

I nodded. "Yes I do."

She nodded too, and then without making a sound, she

started to cry. I think it was first real emotion I had seen from her with none of the diva flamboyance of before, and I reached out and touched her shoulder gently, giving her a little pat and asked if she wanted me to go get Frances. She shook her head, 'no' and took my hand and squeezed it, holding on to it. After a bit she let go, and excusing myself, I quietly left her to her grief.

———

At Bakerwood Winery, it was the same as yesterday with Matt's people processing the grapes, and that lasted most of the morning. When I finally got back to Maverick Cellars to check in on things, Eric had little to say other than, 'Everything's fine, no snags', which I knew from Álvaro, having gotten a full report from him on his cell, that that wasn't entirely true. Eric had insisted that the grapes were coming in too hot from the vineyard and had ordered pellets of dry ice thrown into the bins of grapes to cool them down before they got dumped into the destemmer-crusher. Sound thinking up to a point. Dry ice would certainly cool down the grapes, but if you used too much it also had the unfortunate consequence of freezing the must pump that pushed the crushed grapes into the tank, plugging up the works until everything could be unfrozen again. And this was exactly what happened. I tried not to be amused by this, it must be a fault in my character, but I'll admit I did smile some. Álvaro assured me that Eric hadn't thrown his weight around too much after that, and other than the freezing episode, things had gone smoothly enough, so I decided not to let Eric know I already knew all about it and said to him instead that I was glad to hear there had been no snags.

Gerry Zacks was still on my mind, not having heard back from him yet, so I decided to try phoning again – at his business this time, Future Telecom, Inc. looking up the number in the book. Somebody with a smooth, professional voice I took to be female called an Office Manager, took my call, but no matter how urgently I appealed to her, she wouldn't pass me along to Gerry, and only asked if I wanted to leave a message. I responded that I had already left three messages on his personal phone, but he hadn't gotten back, so if he was there right now, could she please inform him that Chris Garrett from Maverick Cellars was on the phone. She assured me Mr. Zacks would get my message, but that he couldn't come to the phone right then, and the infuriating part was that she wouldn't even admit if he was there and just couldn't come to the phone, or was actually out of the office.

I received a call from Jeff though. He had done some detecting on his end and wanted to know if I was still free for lunch to join him on a little excursion, and I told him I was, so when lunch rolled around I hopped in my truck and headed over to his place.

He was waiting for me, leaning on his squad car when I pulled into his drive, and he got at the passenger door and jumped in. In moments we were back on the road.

"What's up?" I asked.

"Tracked Galbraith to his new address." Off my look, he said, "Thought we might as well pay him a visit. He's got a place east of Napa off the Silverado Trail, so head in that direction."

I did.

"Think he'll talk to us?" I asked.

Jeff shrugged. "Who knows? Won't hurt to try." Then he smiled at me and thumbed at the badge pinned to his chest, "If he thinks this is official all the better."

"Won't hurt," I agreed.

As we drove, my eyes returned now and again to my rear-view mirror and after a bit I saw it, a beat-up white Ford pickup behind us, and it wasn't until that instant that I realized I had been searching the mirrors for that specific truck, only I hadn't been completely aware of it. The realization made my skin prickle. When I was heading to Jeff's place it had been behind me then and there it was again.

Jeff noticed me looking and said, "What?"

"I don't know for sure, but I think that truck's following us."

"What!" Jeff repeated and spun around to look. "Slow down."

I did, and the white pickup seemed to slow down too.

"Pull over to the side of the road," Jeff said, still watching.

I did that too, and the truck still back there a ways slowed down even more until suddenly it whipped off onto a side street and roared out of sight.

I had by now come to a stop next to the road. Traffic continued past us as I turned to look at Jeff.

Jeff said, "You positive about that truck?"

I nodded. "I saw it on my way over to your place."

"Could be a coincidence," he said thinking. "Might not be following you at all."

I nodded. "True, but I can't shake the feeling I've seen that pickup before."

"Before today?"

"Yeah."

"Where?"

"I don't know."

"Well, think!"

"I am!" and I did, reaching back over my memory of the last couple of days, and then I had it. "The first time I saw that truck, it was parked out at the road when I left Bridget Monroe's."

Jeff let loose with some choice words that strongly expressed how he felt. Then he said, "So whoever they are, they've been tailing you for some time."

I used some choice words myself at that point.

Jeff went on, "Tailing. That takes some effort."

I nodded. "Must be pretty curious to know what I'm up to."

"Yeah."

"But is that proof of anything?"

Jeff shook his head. "Nothing to take to the Sheriff. Not yet."

I nodded.

After we both absorbed the ramifications of this new

information we decided to continue on to Galbraith's, and Jeff took up a permanent position watching the road behind us. We didn't catch sight of the truck again the rest of our drive there.

Galbraith's new digs were actually quite a ways off the Silverado Trail, out a twisting stretch of neglected roadway pockmarked with potholes that wound its way into the countryside. The neighboring houses along this stretch were mostly hidden from view by overgrowth, except for a partial glance you got of them as you passed each driveway, and Galbraith's was no different. A galvanized mailbox at the roadside identified the correct address and an opened metal gate held back by an old cinderblock invited us in. The driveway was dirt, and as we caught sight of the place my first thought was Galbraith's new digs didn't look all that new. As a matter of fact the place looked even more overgrown than his neighbors had been, mostly on account of the feeder creek that skirted the near side of the property and eventually dumped a few miles from here into the Napa River. The creek was actually more of a slough that had over time gobbled up most of the yard in the back of the old clapboard house. The house with a porch in front was most likely built sometime in the thirties from the looks of it and badly needed a new coat of paint.

As I brought my truck to a halt, Jeff said, "Quite a step down from high dollar property on Spring Mountain."

I had to agree. I cut the ignition, and as we opened doors and started out, a mangy looking black dog charged ferociously off the porch of the house, growling like it had a mouth full of gravel. The dog was old and as I mentioned, mangy look-ing, and as it drew near I saw it was missing an eye. Before the one-eyed dog could get at my leg and chew it off, a voice boomed out the screen door from the porch, "Booze!"

The dog slowed up, though the growling didn't.

"Booze! Quit that racket!"

The dog, named Booze I deduced, didn't entirely stop but kept coming, but not on account of disregarding the harsh command from the porch. He was just old and sort of bent up from hard living, and slowing down, let alone stopping, didn't happen all at once for him anymore.

The voice from the house, we saw moments later, had come from a rangy looking man maybe a few years older than we were, who came through the screen door and down off the porch.

Booze never came to a stop until he was sniffing intently at my pants, the growls still emanating between the sniffs.

"Don't mind him, he don't bite much anymore," the man said, which didn't relieve me in the slightest.

"Booze! C'mere!"

The dog finally stopped growling and hobbled back toward the porch.

"What can I do you for?" He was eyeing Jeff in his deputy uniform.

Jeff said, "We would like a word with Kenneth Gal-braith."

"That's me, Kenny. What about?"

Jeff and I shared a glance. We had both figured Galbraith

was much older than this guy was.

Jeff clarified, "You're Kenneth Galbraith?"

"Yep."

"You used to own property up on Spring Mountain?"

But now he was shaking his head. "Nope. You'll be wanting my dad, Kenneth Galbraith, Senior. I'm Junior."

One-eyed Booze was back, but this time he wasn't growling, mostly because he obviously had been down to the creek, wet to his chest from brackish water, and had brought back a large river rock nearly as big as his head. He came up to me and dropped the rock on my foot.

"Ouch!"

"He wants you to throw it," Kenny explained.

"It's a rock," I said.

"It's what he likes. Never cared for toys." Kenny waved at the dog, "C'mere, Booze."

Booze picked up the saliva-coated rock and waddled over. Kenny Junior wrestled the slimy chunk out of Booze's mouth and tossed it. The rock looped up in the air, rather higher than I expected and not down into the creek bed where it would've been safer, which was alarming. Booze, easily anticipating the throw, had time to scramble under it like an experienced outfielder and the rock came back down into his outstretched mouth and teeth with a horrendous KLAACCK!

Jeff and I both winced.

"Lookit that damn fool," Kenny Junior laughed. C'mere, Booze." We protested, but Kenny Junior just waved it away as Booze started back with the rock. "It's all right. He don't have much teeth left anyhow." Then he had the rock wrestled away again, and up it went.

KLAACCK!

Jeff and I winced like before.

"C'mere you dumb, stupid mutt."

"Don't throw it again," I said.

"He's all right."

"Don't." I put some weight behind it.

Kenny just shrugged.

"Is your dad around?" Jeff asked, getting back to business, but I knew from his body language that Kenny Junior was dangerously close to getting a rock crammed down his own throat.

"Nope." And Kenny laughed, finding something funny in that.

"Happen to know when he'll be back?"

That question really got a laugh. "He ain't never coming back! He's dead!"

Jeff and I shared another glance.

Kenny Junior was laughing at his joke, but he wasn't amused, you could tell that from his eyes. He gave me a glance and the glance held. "Hey, I know you. You're that guy works at Maverick Cellars."

"Have we met?" I asked.

"Nope. But I know you." His eyes got shrewd, but he didn't elaborate. "What did you want with my old man?"

Jeff pushed past the question and asked, "If you don't mind, could you tell us how your old man died?"

Kenny's eyes remained shrewd. "This is about Vic Miranda croaking, ain't it?"

Jeff nodded.

"Huh, I knew it." He glanced again at me, but returned to Jeff. "You wanna know how my old man died?"

Jeff nodded.

"Well, I'll tell you. Vic killed him," he said with a great deal of venom and then watched us closely to see how we'd react to the news.

I didn't say anything.

Jeff said, "Unlikely."

"That sonofabitch!" Kenny swore. "Might as well have. Dad died from a stroke, on account of what Vic did to him."

"When did he die?"

"Middle of July. He's been dead now four months. What killed him, though, was what Vic did to him. If I'm lying, I'm dying."

"What did Vic do?" I asked.

"Vic stole my Dad's property, that's what."

Chapter

13

Booze sat down in the dirt between us and dropped the rock, the fetching game thankfully at an end. I saw that his tongue was bleeding.

Jeff asked, "How did Vic steal your property?"

"He pulled our grape contract, that's how," Kenny Junior spat. "He knew it would ruin us. Knew we'd lose everything, and he did it on purpose. Just so he could swoop in later and buy our land out from under us."

"You didn't like Vic much, did you?" I said.

"What do you think?" he snarled. "I hated the sonofabitch for what he did."

"Enough to kill him?" Jeff offered.

Kenny Junior lost his snarl. "I thought they said Vic had

153

had an accident."

Jeff made a motion that included me, "We tend to believe different."

Kenny Junior's eyes held on each of us for a moment, and then he nodded. "And maybe I just might've had something to do with it. You'd like that, wouldn't you?"

Jeff shrugged.

Kenny smiled confidently. "Well, I didn't do it."

"That so?"

"I was in New Mexico when Vic died. Just got back yesterday. Check on it, if you want."

"What were you doing in New Mexico?"

"Hunting javalina." Kenny still had his smile going, "Got maybe eight, ten guys'll back me up. Plus the javalina in the freezer." He laughed. "Sorry to disappoint you. Though I can't say I'm all that choked up about Vic dying. Actually, I'm kind of glad he's dead."

I was growing weary of Kenny Junior, and I could see Jeff's face growing redder above his collar, which was dangerous. Between us Booze was still there and had lain down on his side with his bloody tongue flopping out of his mouth into the dirt.

I grabbed Jeff's arm and turned us toward the truck, "C'mon, let's go."

As we drove back to Jeff's place, neither of us talked much. What was there to talk about? Kenneth Galbraith Senior had been dead four months, so as far as that went we had lost another potential suspect. First Patricia, and now Galbraith, and accumulating negatives was fine up to a point, we were making progress of a sort, but it still left us with nothing substantial to hold on to. As far as Galbraith's son, Kenny Junior went, I'll admit I'd be pleased if it turned out he had done it, if for no other reason than that I found him distasteful, but if I had to place a bet right then on whether he had anything to do with Vic's death with only what we already knew, I'd be afraid of taking odds, even one in a million against him, for fear of losing. It wasn't that I believed everything he said. Jeff and I would absolutely check up on all of that, it's just the idea of Kenny doing it didn't pass the smell test. As for his opinion that Vic killed his father, well, that stunk even worse. No bet. I didn't need to see Jeff pinching his nose to know what he thought. His silence was enough. No sense stating the obvious, so we didn't. On top of that, neither of us the whole way back got another glimpse of the white pickup.

I did get a call from Tony Picozzi on my cell. Apparently they had lost the hitch pin on the tractor. The pin kept the tractor and trailer attached together and they couldn't pull any more bins full of fruit from the vineyard to the loading area without another pin and would I bring them one from the winery. So after I had dropped Jeff off, I stopped in at Maverick Cellars and scrounged around for one and was almost ready to go to the tractor dealer and buy another cockamamie pin, when I finally found the spare I was looking for and headed with it up Spring Mountain.

My mind wasn't on tractors and hitch pins, though, as I drove up out of the Valley on the curving Spring Mountain

Road. It was on Vic, a man I had thought I knew well, somebody I had worked for, had admired and respected, had pat-
terned my career after to a great extent. Vic had been more
to me than just my boss, he had been both my mentor and
my friend, but how could I admire and respect a man that
was an adulterer and maybe a land swindler?

I hadn't expected to run up against Vic's shortcomings. I
had made it my job to dig into his past and uncover whatever
was there that may have led to his death, and usually in such
instances if you dig deep enough, you find at the bottom some
rather nasty business. I just hadn't been prepared for that nasty
business to speak directly to Vic's character, especially since
I had made it my job to defend that character to the outside
world. I guess I was just feeling a little let down. Or maybe I
just wished Vic were still around to explain his behavior.

When I got to the vineyard, I had expected to see everybody standing around waiting for me to show up with the
much-needed pin, but I was mistaken. Tony had his crew in
full swing picking what was left to pick on the last couple of
rows, and rolling slowly along between those rows was the
tractor clearly hitched to the trailer pulling full bins of fruit
toward the loading area. I parked my truck under the shade
of a madrone near the fence line, cut the ignition and hopped
out, not forgetting to grab the hitch pin as I did.

"Paisano!" Tony yelled, having seen me drive up. He was
walking next to the tractor that was crawling steadily along.

I waved, jumped the fence, and headed in that direction.
When I got close, I held up the pin for Tony to see, and he

just shrugged.

"We found the one we lost," he said.

"I see that."

"Had everybody walk up and down the rows looking," Tony said, and smiled. "We got lucky." Then he reached for the pin I had, and I handed it over. "I'll keep this with the tractor, for the future."

"Save me a trip next time," I said.

Tony stopped at my tone and regarded me for a moment. "What's the matter, now?"

I looked at Tony's concerned, weather-beaten face and decided to confide in him. "I went to talk with Galbraith today."

Tony's eyes widened. "That's hard to do."

"Yeah, since Galbraith's pushing up daisies. I didn't know he had died from a stroke four months ago."

Tony was nodding, apparently he had already known.

"So I talked with his son instead."

"Still having trouble with Vic's accident?" Tony asked.

"Having trouble with Vic, period," I said and proceeded to fill him in on what Jeff and I had learned on our brief visit with Kenny Junior. Finishing up with the accusations Kenny had made of Vic's land grab, Tony just waved it away.

"Forget it," he said. "Galbraith was a fool, and obviously so is his son. They lost their property long before Vic pulled out. Vic had stuck with them long after all the other wineries had given up." Then Tony chuckled. "Of course, Kenny didn't tell you the real reason Vic pulled out. His old man backed his tractor into Vic's truck! On purpose!"

"No kidding?"

"That was the last straw. Vic was so pissed, that right then he cancelled their grape contract."

"What about Vic buying the land out from under them."

"That was Zacks. Zacks was looking for property. Looking for a way into the wine biz. You should talk with Benny about that."

I nodded.

"Vic never had designs on their land. He always thought Maverick Cellars was large enough as it was."

"So why not blame Zacks?"

"Everybody in the Valley knew Maverick Cellars meant Vic, and Vic, Maverick Cellars, whether the money came from Zacks or not. Vic was the easy target."

As I absorbed this, Tony clapped me on the back, which sort of stung to be honest, though he had taken the sting out of Vic's actions for me concerning Galbraith's property. What Tony had said fit much better with what I had remembered about Vic's behavior. Then smiling big, Tony said conspiratorially, "C'mere. Since you made the trip up the mountain, I wanna show you something." He made me catch up with the tractor still hauling the bins of picked fruit toward the loading area. Then he selected out a cluster of grapes as the tractor continued rolling along and held it out for my inspection. He motioned at the rows behind us, climbing up the hill, his eyes twinkling. "This is what we're getting at the top."

Tony handed over the cluster, and I inspected. The berries

were small, very small and as I held the grapes in my hand, the skins felt soft and silky, almost velvety to the touch. The smell of them was sweet and ripe and mouthwatering. I was glad they had netted the trellises, because grapes smelling this good would have brought the birds like ringing the dinner bell.

Tony's eyes were still twinkling. "Go ahead. Taste."

I did, and I wouldn't have been surprised to hear that my eyes were twinkling as well. "Oh, my God!" I said.

Tony was smiling very big. "See? What did I tell you?"

"Yes, I see," I said. Though he hadn't told me anything with words necessarily, we were sure communicating — only it was the grapes that were doing all the talking. I gave him some of the berries from the cluster, and we both tasted the fruit together. The flavor was just immense, but in no way over ripe — dark and rich and thrillingly lip smacking, especially when I imagined what kind of wine I could make out of it.

"This was why Vic stuck with Galbraith when no one else would."

Tony nodded. "He could see the potential."

So could I, and my mind raced ahead, thinking about what I wanted to do with this fruit.

"I would love to keep this lot separated," I told Tony.

"I knew you would. That's why I've already had it done!"

"Paisano!" I said and this time slapped Tony on the back.

Later, heading down Spring Mountain Road, I was still thinking about Vic and the grapes Tony had miraculously grown on property most everybody else had relegated to the compost pile. Vic would've been just as excited as I was over the quality of the fruit, especially knowing what shape the vineyard had been in when they had started working with it. Turning things around in only three short years was what had made it so impressive. I smiled to myself, thinking how Matt Bakerwood would probably react when this lot came in. Green with envy I was sure. I'd have to keep my eye on him, or he'll be siphoning off this lot and filling his own barrels with it, if I wasn't careful.

Careful was what I should have been, though, as I was rolling through the tight turns and twists of the road coming down off the mountain — maybe I would have seen the white pickup before it had come up so close behind me. I don't exactly know what drew my eyes, but I glanced into my rearview mirror and there it was, filling the glass, right up on my bumper. Before I could feed my engine more gas, the white pickup was gunning its engine, and I felt more than heard the collision of metal against metal as our bumpers met and the back end of my truck lurch and lose traction. "Goddammit!" I said in anger. I had been rammed! The back end of my vehicle screeched sideways, and as I pitched off the asphalt onto the gravel shoulder I tried to straighten back out by turning the steering wheel hard in the other direction, but all I managed to do was straighten myself directly off the road. The road embankment fell away sharply, and as my truck plowed through the road railing and pitched heavily into the air, I remembered thinking I had been lucky to have narrowly missed slamming those two trees growing right next to the road, and then I was zooming past them sailing forty feet above the trellised vines of Cabernet Franc which were holding on precariously by their roots to the side of the mountain. The tail end of my truck seemed to want to pass the front and was heading steadily over my cab when I finally came back to earth. I tried to brace myself by gripping tightly to the steering wheel and locking my arms, but it must not have done any good, because at impact, in a fury of metallic noise and breaking glass everything went black.

Chapter 14

I AWOKE WITH a start. Behind echoes of clashing metal and cracking glass, somebody was knocking lightly at my bedroom door and when my eyes sprang open and were finally able to focus I recognized immediately it was Rosalynd. Seeing Rosalynd standing at my door knocking was certainly surprising, but not as surprising as finding myself not in my bedroom at all, but from the medical apparatus and charts and bed curtains hung from the ceiling and the antiseptic smells, I was in the hospital, though the realization didn't penetrate the heavy fog of my brain right away. I'm sure I looked as bewildered as I felt sitting there in bed gawking, because Rosalynd suddenly giggled at me and came over quickly and sat on the bed.

"Don't tell me you still can't remember anything?" She took up my hand in hers and gave it a squeeze, and though my brains were scrambled I didn't fail to notice how soft and warm hers were.

"Wha—" My tongue wasn't hooked up properly yet.

"You're at Queen of the Valley."

"Yeah, I got that," I managed thickly.

Her face brightened. "You do?"

I motioned at the room, which was obviously a hospital room and asked, "What happened?"

Her face fell, "You still don't remember."

"Remember?"

"You were in an accident."

"An accident?"

"You were in a car wreck," Rosalynd explained patiently and waited to see if any of this was ringing a bell. Apparently my bell had been rung sufficiently enough already, because it wasn't, so she said, "You hit your head pretty hard."

I removed my hand from hers and discovered the bandages wrapped around my head. "Well, that explains the jackhammering going on behind my eyeballs."

"You've been in the hospital two days."

"Two days!" I exclaimed, coming out of bed.

Rosalynd smiled and pushed me gently back against the bed pillows. Then she explained, as my truck had made impact once more with the earth after leaving Spring Mountain Road, apparently my forehead had continued onward until it too had made impact with the steering wheel, hard enough to bend it nearly in half and also put a handsome gash into the meat above my brow. The blow not only knocked me for a loop, it knocked me loopy, and goofy, and silly, and senseless, and nearly into next week. That was why I was having trouble remembering anything.

I nodded, remembering, "Yeah, antegrade and retrograde amnesia."

"You remember you've had amnesia?"

"Sure," I said. It was my turn to smile. "I also remember Doc Matulich's technical explanation of causality yesterday afternoon," and at Rosalynd's look of wonder, I launched into what the Doc had told me about retrograde amnesia being the memory loss before the casual event (my crash) and antegrade amnesia being the memory loss for what happened afterward. My remembering Doc Matulich's explanation yesterday afternoon had both of us beaming.

"I remember the CT scan results too," I said. "Even though my concussion was pretty serious, there had been no internal hemorrhages or brain bruises, so with time I should make a full recovery."

"And here you are recovering!"

"Yeah!" I said.

We were still beaming when Jeff's voice boomed from the doorway, "Find any loose marbles rolling around?"

"As a matter of fact," Rosalynd said still beaming, "I think we just did," and reported to Jeff what I had just remembered.

"Yeah?" Jeff brightened. He had a brown grocery bag full

of stuff and a carton holding two cups of hot coffee carefully gripped in one hand while with the other hand he grabbed at a chair from the far wall and pulled it close. "I knew all Chris needed was a good night's sleep."

"Here, let me help you," Rosalynd said to Jeff, taking the cups of coffee from him.

"Thanks, darling," Jeff said and got the chair in place and dropped into it while also dropping the grocery bag of stuff at the foot of my bed.

Darling?

I watched as Rosalynd returned to Jeff one of the coffees and sat back on the bed with the other one. I looked back and forth between the two of them, watched as they both took sips of the java and smiled at one another. Clearly more had happened during the last two days of blackness than I was currently aware.

Darling?

"Maybe somebody oughta fill me in on what's been going on around here," I said.

Jeff swallowed some coffee and said, "That's a good idea. Like what, for instance?"

"Like, I don't know, because I can't remember."

Rosalynd giggled. "Well, you've been acting pretty goofy lately."

"Goofy?" I prompted.

Jeff laughed and then imitating me said, "Where's my pants?"

Rosalynd joined him with a laugh. "That's right. That's

how we knew something had happened to your memory. You kept asking everybody, 'Where's my pants?' over and over."

"Where's my pants?" Jeff chortled. "You could never remember!"

"Well, where the heck are my pants?" I asked.

"Oh, no," Rosalynd said, biting her lip. "He's regressing."

"I'm not regressing," I said, taking a candid peek beneath the bed sheets. "In point of fact, I'm currently, as we sit here reminiscing, without drawers." As Rosalynd's eyes flashed in response to the news, I went on, "Yeah, better take care, darling. There's only a thin sheet separating the two of us."

"Relax," Jeff said, motioning at the sack on the floor. "I stopped by your place this morning and brought a change of clothes."

"Well, where're the pants I was wearing when I was brought in here?" I asked again. "I vaguely recall something happening to them."

"They had to cut them off," Rosalynd explained like she'd had to do so many times already. "All your clothes actually."

"In E.R. that's standard procedure," Jeff said, and added, "Hope they didn't have any sentimental value."

They didn't as far as I could remember, so I waved it away. "What else?"

Rosalynd resumed, "You remember what you said to the Doctor when he was examining your head wound?"

"No."

She giggled. "You asked if the stitches would leave a scar, would he shape them like a lightning bolt."

I touched the bandages circling my head, smiling, "Well, did he?"

Rosalynd smiled back at me, "You'll just have to wait and see."

Jeff and Rosalynd then filled me in on the rest of what had been happening over the last few days, how a parade of people and friends and well-wishers had come to visit, including even the Mirandas, minus Eric of course, and I remembered most of it. Jeff told me he had called my folks and filled them in on what happened and assured them I would be all right, and I made a note to myself get ahold of them later. I remembered Marjorie visiting and how upset she had been seeing me lying in bed with giant raccoon eyes, which Rosalynd said were looking much better now having had a couple days to heal. I remembered without any prompting, Álvaro coming and Tony and Henri and the others from work, and Benny who had told me not to worry about Maverick Cellars, that Eric was helping out nicely and Matt Bakerwood was also filling in since he was already aware of Maverick Cellars' house style, so I didn't have to concern myself with anything at work and should just get some rest, which of course, as soon as I remembered my job again, I started to really worry. For more than two days Eric and Matt had been watching over my wine? Egad! I had to get out of bed. And in a hurry!

But nothing happens in a hospital in a hurry, so I was told rather forcefully by Rosalynd to lean back and relax, the Doctor had to release me first and that meant he had to examine me again before he would do so, so I wasn't going anywhere anytime soon, there was nothing that could be done about it. Jeff backed her up too, which got my mind back on a question I had had earlier.

I narrowed my eyes at Rosalynd. "By the way," I said, "How did you know I was in a car wreck? I remember the last I heard you were headed back to the City."

There was amusement dancing in her eyes again that I had become so familiar with. "I did head back," she said.

"To San Francisco?"

"Yes."

I looked at Jeff. "Did you call her?"

"Nope."

"So how?"

"You wouldn't believe me if I told you," Rosalynd said, her eyes twinkling.

"Try me."

"All right. Patricia Miranda told me."

She was right I didn't believe it. "Patricia called you?"

"She thought I would be — concerned."

Patricia had told her? The mother of Eric? The person who had had Rosalynd dating her son? I tried to sort that out, but had to finally set it aside unsorted until my brains unscrambled further.

I adjusted the bandages on my forehead. The truth was I was actually feeling pretty good — better than good now that the missing days had mostly come back. I could recall nearly everything clear back, right up to — when all at once everything finally did come back, the white pickup, the rear-ending, the leaving the road, the failed attempt at truck-flying, and the crash! I winced.

Rosalynd squeezed my hand with concern. "Is your bandage too tight?"

"No," I said and shook my head, taking care not to move too abruptly. That wince wasn't from the pain. I had only just recalled the troubling last words I had uttered as I was leaving the road and nearly leaving this existence — Goddamnit! Not the best choice in hindsight, especially if I had landed not on the mountainside, but before Saint Peter at the Pearly Gates. I waved away her questions. "I was just recalling — my accident."

"What?" Jeff said, straightening up in his chair. "You remember your accident?"

"Yeah."

"That's wonderful," Rosalynd said, beaming.

"Only it wasn't an accident," I said. "I was run off the road."

—❦—

"The white pickup," Jeff growled as we sped along in Rosalynd's convertible, his voice elevated over the wind. "It had to be the white pickup!"

Jeff was in the back seat, I was in the passenger's seat and Rosalynd was driving up Spring Mountain Road returning us to the scene of the crash, and much too fast in my opinion.

"Could you slow down?" I asked, trying to apply the brakes on my side of the floorboard and of course not finding any.

"I'm going ten miles under the speed limit as it is," she

protested, but slowed down anyway.

"It feels like we're flying!" My eyes had the tendency, I noticed, to leap straight off the sides of the road as we sped along, and I couldn't help imagining us plummeting into the creek bottom below, so I tried watching the sky instead, which was easy since Rosalynd had the convertible's top down.

"This white pickup," Rosalynd said over the whine of her down shifting, bringing us back to topic, "had been following you?"

I nodded, and Jeff quickly brought her up to speed on all of that. "So we can safely assume," he said summing up, "that since Chris' accident wasn't an accident, Vic's wasn't either."

"You mean whoever was driving the white pickup also killed Vic?"

"More than likely," Jeff said.

Rosalynd nodded, though she wasn't smiling like before. If anything she looked grim. "I don't like it."

"It was the white pickup," I assured her. "I'm remembering that correctly."

"No, it's not that. I don't like that somebody's out there right now trying to kill you."

"Yeah, I don't like that either," Jeff echoed.

I nodded, not liking the idea much myself.

"Before, when you were looking into Vic's death," Rosalynd went on, "I thought it was so exciting. Now I just want you to stop."

"Oh, Chris won't stop now," Jeff said to her with certainty, shaking his head for added emphasis. "Maybe before if nothing had come of it he might've dropped the whole thing, but not after being run off the road and nearly killed. No way. I've known him too long to believe that."

Rosalynd was looking at me, "Is that true? You're planning to keep charging wildly ahead?"

I shrugged. "I am," I said, "as long as we keep below ten miles an hour."

Jeff laughed, but Rosalynd didn't.

"This isn't funny," she said.

"I know it's not."

"I don't like it."

"I know you don't."

The air blowing around in the car gave me the feeling my bandages were at any moment going to shoot off in the wind, so I had to hold onto them to keep them steady, though it wasn't too much longer before we reached the spot where we were headed with the two trees close together and the damaged road railing.

Rosalynd found an area wide enough off the road to park and did so, and we hopped out and crossed over to the other side where bright orange hazard cones and some makeshift scaffolding kept the traffic out of harm's way. The three of us stood for a moment at the break in the railing and looked down the mountain at the divots in the ground made by my truck and the uprooted grapevines and torn out trellises. The distance was farther than I had remembered.

Jeff said, "From where your tire treads left the roadway, right here," he pointed, "to where you again made impact with the side of the mountain, way over there," he pointed again, "was measured to be over a hundred and thirty-three feet! Which, I might add, was farther than the Wright Brothers' first recorded flight in their bi-plane at Kitty Hawk. Only you did it in a '66 Chevy pickup. Quite a feat."

"I'm amazed I survived," I said, measuring the distance with my eyes and marveling. I felt Rosalynd's hand slip into mine.

Jeff resumed, "When paramedics arrived on the scene, you were still behind the wheel and apparently wide awake, which was lucky since if you had been found unconscious they would've stuck a breathing tube down your throat and that's never pleasant. You were pretty bloody from your head wound, and clearly out of your gourd."

"No doubt."

"You couldn't tell anybody what had happened, so everybody had assumed you had lost control yourself, but now we know different."

"Yes, we do," I said, and felt Rosalynd's hand squeeze mine.

"So, now what do you want to do?" Jeff asked.

"I want to see my truck."

My truck was at the County Impound lot, and I was struck again by how much my memory was off from the reality of what had happened, and I was amazed again I had survived. From the front grill to the cab, it looked just like a giant accordion with all the air pressed out. The front windshield was gone, as well as the two side windows, but the back one was surprisingly still intact, only the truck's frame was nearly bent into a 'U' with a great deal of dirt, grapevines and trellis material still wedged into various pieces and parts. Looking inside the cab made me wonder how I had kept from getting my legs crushed.

"You know," I said just to be saying something, "this truck used to belong to my Dad."

"It must've meant a lot to you," Rosalynd said.

I nodded. "I remember how he used to baby it. I always tried to do likewise, but now look at it."

"I think we can fix it, Chris," Jeff said, which made me laugh for some reason.

"You think?"

Jeff laughed too, because there was no way in hell that truck would ever fly again, "Yep, a little elbow grease here and there and in a jiffy—"

"A jiffy?"

Well, a couple jiffies anyway," he let the absurdity sink in and Rosalynd joined us in the laugh. "So, now what do you want to do?" Jeff finally asked.

"I'm hungry," I said. "I haven't eaten anything but Jell-O for over two days. Let's go eat."

"Sounds good."

"What're you hungry for?" Rosalynd asked.

I thought about it. "A hamburger."

Whenever I went camping, or fishing or was out roughing it in the wilderness away from civilization for an extended period, it wasn't a hot shower that I missed most, or a comfortable bed, or a blessed reprieve from the pesky bugs, it was hamburgers. Hamburgers and fries to be exact — don't forget the fries. For some reason, hamburgers and fries more than anything else to me meant comfort. So that was what I ordered, a hamburger with bacon and cheese, fries, and a cup of coffee.

We had stopped at a burger joint off Highway 29, and Rosalynd had decided to follow suit and go for the bacon burger and fries too. Jeff got a Reuben with extra onions, and an iced tea, without the ice, which made it just tea, I pointed out to him. He said he didn't want hot tea, and that was what they'd have given him if he had just ordered tea, and he preferred his tea cold, and hopefully not tepid.

"I can't abide tepid tea," he said, shaking his head.

"What do you want to drink?" I asked Rosalynd. "A soda?"

"No, lemonade please. I'm not much for soda."

"Yeah, neither is Chris," Jeff said, helpfully pointing out our commonality.

Off Rosalynd's raised brows, I said, "It's the sweetness and artificial flavors. They tend to muddle the palate."

"Oh. For me, I don't like the bubbles."

"'Cause they tickle your nose?"

"No," she said, making a face. "They make me burp. Have you ever tried to hold back a burp?"

Before I could say, 'Not really,' Jeff piped up with, "Oh, yeah, yeah, very painful," and grimaced in agreement with

175

her. Coming from him, I had to laugh. I had often heard him eruct in one long continuous chorus the whole Star Spangled Banner.

We paid the bill and they gave us a buzzer that would vibrate once our order was ready and we could then go retrieve it, so we found a table in back on the grass to wait. Rosalynd excused herself and left for the ladies room, and I finally had Jeff to myself and took the opportunity to ask him about something that had been nagging me all day.

"So, why the change of heart? The last time I checked, you thought she was a double agent."

"Rosalynd?" He nodded and gave me an amused, but measured look. "A lot has happened in the last couple days."

"So I've heard — and mostly remembered." I motioned at him, "Tell me."

So he did. He told me about how I had been brought in to the hospital and how I had been made to wait to get in to see a doctor in the E.R. and how Rosalynd had rushed in and found me still covered in blood from head wound to toe, and when she discovered how long we had been waiting, she hit the roof. "She immediately got on the phone and talked with her family," Jeff said, "and her family apparently has some pull because it wasn't too much longer before Doctor Matulich, the best head trauma specialist on the West Coast, I learned later, arrived by helicopter from San Francisco."

I marveled at Jeff's story. "She did all that?"

"She did, and made sure you got the very best care possible.

She was a tiger! Ferocious!" Jeff smiled at the memory. "We also had a lot of time on our hands the last couple days to visit and get to know one another, waiting to see if you'd ever snap out of it or remain a lame-brain."

"But why did she do it? It wasn't guilt?"

Jeff looked at me funny, "No, you lame-brain! You must've cracked your egg worst that I thought. Isn't it obvious? She likes you!"

Oh, I thought.

"I kind of like her too," I admitted.

"So you're not a lame-brain after all."

Chapter 15

I HADN'T FORGOTTEN about Maverick Cellars. I still wanted to get back and check on Eric and Matt and see how they were handling my wine. After nearly three days' absence, I was imagining all sorts of calamities taking place, but after recalling the white pickup, my winemaking concerns had to be temporarily put on hold. Now that we finally had something that maybe brought into doubt the theory that Vic's drowning was purely accidental, it was more important to get the authorities up to speed on it as quickly as possible and that meant paying a visit to Sheriff Coulette.

Jeff had learned the Sheriff wasn't at the office, but had taken the afternoon off and was probably home, so that was where we headed. We needed to talk with him in person, since what we had to tell him wasn't something to leave with subordinates or speak idly over the phone. Rosalynd was feeling fatigued after enduring all the excitement over the last couple of days, and instead of going with us had decided to head for the place in Stag's Leap where she was staying, and freshen up and maybe take a nap. I could've used a nap myself, to be honest, but talking with the Sheriff shouldn't be put off any longer. We had agreed to meet up later this evening with Rosalynd, if both Jeff and I would promise to keep safe and stay out of trouble, and both of us assured her we'd be very careful. She had dropped us at my place where Jeff had parked his Jeep. Then the two of us proceeded to Sheriff Coulette's house, which was in the hills on the way to Angwin.

As it turned out we were lucky and managed to catch the Sheriff still at home, but just barely. He had his Dodge pickup hitched to a bass boat in the driveway, loaded up for an easy afternoon of lake fishing. Sitting in the boat putting in rods and readying tackle were two children I assumed belonged to the Sheriff, a boy around ten or eleven, and his baby sister probably not quite seven. Jeff pulled the Jeep in next to the boat and shut off the engine and we hopped out.

We waved and said 'hello' to the kids, who were eyeing us suspiciously. "What a great day for fishing!" Jeff went on with enthusiasm. "Of course, what day isn't great when you're going fishing, huh?"

The children didn't respond. They seemed preoccupied with my bandages and facial bruising, so I explained, "I was in a car wreck."

Jeff and I stepped up to the boat and put our forearms on the gunwale and saw the boy was arranging lures in a tackle box, and Jeff, being friendly said, "Hey, I got a lure just like that one! Let me see," and as he reached for the jig the boy handed it carefully over. "Yeah, ooh, just like it. Only mine has stripes instead of spots like this one, and it has three sets of hooks, not two, and it's shorter, not quite as fat as this, and mine's a different color."

The boy was looking at Jeff like he had two heads, instead of just one, when his little sister piped up with, "That's not the same!"

Jeff laughed. Then he said to her, "Do you like to fish?"

With Jeff's attention on her, the little girl turned suddenly shy, so all he got was a small nod.

"Chris and I love to fish. Love it! Don't we, Chris?"

I didn't remember ever professing my love, but I went along anyway and said, "You bet."

"We're fishing fanatics!" he said straight to both of them. "We're really into it. Nuts about fishing. There's nothing we don't know about the subject. Nothing! Even thought about becoming fishing guides. Go ahead, Chris, tell us about the last time you went fishing. Go on."

"Jeff," I said, stammering, "I haven't been fishing in over a year. I can't even remember the last time I went. I've been way too busy."

"Yeah," Jeff admitted awkwardly, "Me too."

It was then Sheriff Coulette emerged from the house, a two-story wood-shingled suburban monster tucked back against the trees with an attached triple-wide garage. He lumbered across the lawn toward the boat carrying a large ice chest heavy with easy afternoon fishing essentials (for novices, that's sandwiches, sodas and beer) when he caught sight of us. Upon recognition, I saw him hitch a step before coming the rest of the way and stowing the heavy chest into the back of the boat. He said, "Garrett, you look like hell."

"I sort of feel that way too," I said back to him, touching the bandages.

He gave a glance at Jeff, who was still looking at fishing lures with the children.

"Then what're you doing here?" he growled. "Shouldn't you be in bed?"

"Probably," I admitted, "but I thought you should know — I was run off the road."

So I filled him in on the white pickup and about being tailed by it over the last few days, and about how Jeff and I had been poking around on our own, and what we had found out, which from the way the Sheriff's face reddened at the news I figured I better move on as quickly as I could to how I came suddenly to leave Spring Mountain Road. I finished by describing the white pickup.

He was looking narrowly at me. "This just come to you, I take it?"

I shrugged. "I was conked pretty hard in the head."

"Uh-huh. What else?"

"Nothing else, except it brings Vic's supposed accident into question."

The Sheriff made a noise. "I don't see that."

"Then why else would somebody want to run me off the road?"

"Maybe it was unintentional."

"Unintentional? After tailing me for who knows how long? Not because I was looking into Vic's death or asking too many questions?"

The Sheriff glared at me. "I'm still not convinced you didn't run off that road on your own, Garrett."

Jeff, still with the children, but I noticed carefully following our conversation, was admiring a fishing rod the little girl was showing him. "Ooh, wow, look at that!" he said, like discovering real treasure. "Do you know what that is?" He fingered the pole reverently as the girl nodded that she knew. "Do you? Yeah, it's genuine – baboon!"

The Sheriff shot his deputy a look, but Jeff mostly had his back to his boss, so the Sheriff wasn't sure.

The Sheriff's daughter giggled and said to Jeff, "No it's not, it's bamboo!"

Jeff laughed.

The Sheriff looked back levelly at me and said, "Patricia told me you had stopped by her place for a visit." Before I could say, 'I'd been invited', he put up a hand, "Now, I don't know how you persuaded her, but my sister's now convinced somebody murdered her husband."

"She is?"

"Yeah, but I'm not."

"But you'll look into the white pickup?"

The Sheriff looked back at his children who were having fun with Jeff. After a long moment watching them, he sighed heavily. "You say it was a hit-and-run? That's a serious crime. I'll look into it."

As Jeff drove us back to his place, he said, "Don't think Coulette isn't rethinking Vic's death. He's not a fool. No matter how he acts sometimes. Your hit-and-run gives him the perfect opportunity to look into both situations at the same time, without stirring up too much political dust."

I nodded, fully aware of the political pressures Coulette was under. I just didn't have Jeff's conviction the Sheriff would reopen the investigation into his brother-in-law's death without more to go on than what little hearsay I had given him. Not yet anyway.

Jeff could see I wasn't convinced, so he said, "Of course, that doesn't mean we stop our own investigation."

"What, look for the white pickup along with the Sheriff?"

"No. The Sheriff's perfectly capable of handling that — I was thinking about something else, actually somebody else."

I thought for a moment and then had it too. "Gerry Zacks."

"Yep. Gerry Zacks," Jeff echoed. "His name has popped up way too many times to be ignored any longer. And the fact that he's been incommunicado this whole time makes me very suspicious."

I was nodding, "Yeah, me too. Time we had a little talk with ol' Ger."

So I tried again on my cell to reach Zacks at Future Telecom, but the same friendly female voice I had heard before once more put up the professional block, and was she ever good at it. For some reason, she made it seem that Gerry was just down the hall, only he was way too busy at the moment to break away from whatever important business he was currently engaged in to speak with anyone, nothing personal, and that he would definitely get the message that I had called and would certainly call back just as soon as it was humanly possible, she was eminently aware of how important my call was and continued with more of the same until I maybe got a little testy with her — pointing out if the future of telecommunications meant never talking with the person you were attempting to reach, then they were doing a bang-up job over there. Of course that ended the conversation real quick, but I was through with it anyway.

"Maybe we're going about this all wrong," Jeff said after I hung up.

"What do you mean?"

"The direct approach isn't working. Maybe we should come at him in a round about way."

"Like, for instance?"

"For instance, isn't Zacks a rather prominent business personality?"

"Yeah?"

"Then there's gotta be a lot of stuff about him on the Internet. Who knows what we might turn up?"

I nodded, "Couldn't hurt."

So once we got to Jeff's apartment, Jeff hopped to it on his computer and started accessing the web, while I hopped, or rather eased onto his couch, feeling sort of caved in from all the activity since leaving the hospital, and propped my head carefully on the cushioned arm and took a break.

Jeff had an impressive collection of computer hardware cluttering up one wall of his apartment, with cables and terminals, and routers and firewalls, and various devices and other hacker stuff that I didn't even pretend to know anything about, though Jeff had tried patiently to explain to me on numerous occasions what everything did and what it was for, but his explanations always got too technical to follow along closely, so mostly I ended up just nodding and pointing out that his hobby was turning into an obsession. He would just laugh, being all too familiar with my own obsession — wine grapes.

I watched him from the couch, his back to me, the clicking of the keyboard as he typed various commands lulling me peacefully back against the cushions, and yawned and relaxed and even closed my eyes — when I heard the front door open abruptly. I looked up to see Jeff coming in with a load of mail in his hands.

"Get a good rest?" he asked, flipping idly through the mail.

I blinked and rubbed my eyes. "How long have I been out?"

"Couple hours, that's all. Though you'd expect a cord of wood to be stacked up from all the sawing."

I smiled. "That bad, huh?"

He just grinned, and tossed the mail on the coffee table.
"So what'd you find out?"

"Well, I found out Gerry Zacks has had some very high
highs, and some very low lows."

"Meaning?"

"Meaning his business Future Telecom was flying high
in the late nineties before the dot-com crash." Jeff went on,
"Apparently like many other technology stocks, Future Telecom
took a tumble, but that wasn't the worst of it. Their basic business — setting up phone information systems for companies
and networks also got hit with the double-whammy when the
popularity of cell phones took off."

"You'd think being the future of telecommunications,
they'd have seen that coming."

"Uh-huh, that's what everybody thought. That's when
Future Telecom started being referred to as FuTel for short."

"Ouch," I said. "I always thought that was raw."

"It was meant to be." Jeff resumed, "Lately, the business has
turned to fiber optics, both in this country and abroad, but
the competition in that area is fierce, and though nobody is
completely privy to how the company is really doing, rumors
abound."

"What about his Internet business?"

Jeff nodded, "Future Vacations. That was another attempt
at diversification — upscale vacations for the rich and super
rich, with a fleet of yachts and jets and even a submarine at
their disposal. Apparently anything anybody wants isn't off
limits, from a journey to the bottom of the sea, to the heavens

above aboard a Russian rocket."

"Sounds impressive."

"They also have various leases on mansions and chateaus in the best locations around the world, some even here in Napa Valley, but this is where things turn sour. Rumor has it, Future Vacations is on the brink of bankruptcy."

"How did you learn that off the Internet?"

Jeff smiled deviously. "You'd be surprised what you can find if you know where to look."

"And if you know how to look."

"Precisely," Jeff said, the corner of a smile showing. "Also, I did a credit search."

"So where does this leave us? I don't suppose that thing," I pointed at his computer, "can tell us how to get Gerry Zacks to answer his phone?"

"Not likely. But we're more informed."

"And," I said, keeping upbeat, "we know Zacks is currently under some financial pressure."

"Money is always an excellent motive for murder."

I agreed. "And we still have the round about approach."

Jeff's eyebrows lifted. He knew me well enough to know I had thought of something. Maybe it had come to me in my sleep.

"We need to get at Gerry Zacks, right?" I said.

"Right," he said.

"And since we can't get at him, maybe we can get at somebody close to him."

"Yeah," Jeff nodded, following along, "who then might get

at him for us."

"That's right."

"Like who?"

"Like somebody who runs in the kinds of circles guys like Gerry Zacks run in."

"Got somebody in mind?"

"Yep, since she's no longer a double agent."

"Rosalynd," Jeff said, finally catching up.

I smiled at him. "Good idea?"

Jeff shrugged. "Couldn't hurt."

So I called Rosalynd and told her how to find Jeff's apartment. She said she'd be right over and when she arrived, looking as fresh as spring flowers from her nap and after giving both of us hugs and smiles at remaining safe and sound, looked around quizzically and then abruptly asked Jeff, "Where's your kitchen?"

Jeff said, "Don't have one."

She looked at both of us accusatorily, "I thought you said you were gourmet chefs. How can you be a gourmet chef without a kitchen?"

Obviously she had a point. Jeff chuckled awkwardly. Glancing at me he managed to stammer, "Uh–"

"Well," I said, coming to his rescue, "Jeff makes a mean spaghetti."

Jeff quickly nodded, "Yep, with my coffee pot."

He pointed proudly at the drip-coffee maker on a portable counter.

Rosalynd's eyes narrowed suspiciously, "You make spaghetti

in your coffee pot?"

"You know, I've often thought of adding a little coffee to my spaghetti sauce," I said, reflecting on its merits. "It adds that intriguing touch of flavor you just can't quite place."

Jeff was nodding, "That's right. Gour-o-met!"

Rosalynd was looking at both of us dubiously. "Yeah, I bet."

Jeff and I both shrugged.

Rosalynd went on, "So, why am I here?"

I said, "Well, we need your help."

"God knows you do."

"We can't seem to get to Gerry Zacks."

Jeff and I then filled her in with all we knew about Gerry Zacks and Future Telecom and what we had just learned on the Internet. After we were through, I asked if she could help us.

"We wondered if maybe you knew somebody, who knew Gerry—" I said.

"Or might know somebody," Jeff cut in, "that knew somebody that could get us in to see Gerry."

"Or who could tell us where Gerry Zacks is currently hiding," I finished.

Rosalynd looked back and forth between us thinking and then said, "You'll want to talk with D.H."

"Who?" Jeff asked.

"D.H. Hackett," she said nodding with satisfaction. "Yep, he's perfect. He owns six or seven businesses, knows everybody. He's just the sort of person who might know how to get to Gerry Zacks."

"Think he'll help us?" I said.

She shrugged. "We can only ask. But I don't see why not. Our family has known D.H. for years." Then she said, "I can't believe you haven't met D.H. — *Can you hack it?*"

"Can you hack it?" I asked, not knowing if I had heard correctly.

Rosalynd nodded. "A nickname of sorts. Because he's so difficult to keep pace with. He's a real dynamo." Then she smiled and I saw that twinkling in her eyes. "Oh, you're gonna love D.H."

Chapter 16

ROSALYND CALLED HOME and had somebody, I didn't catch who exactly, find D.H. Hackett's number for her and then hung up and proceeded to call him, but got a busy signal and had to leave a message. It was only a few minutes later that D.H. returned her call. He said he was catching a plane this evening for the East Coast, but if it was urgent he was currently in the vicinity and if I could meet right now, he could squeeze me in. Rosalynd asked me if this was all right, and I said, "It's perfect," and that was why we were standing out front of Jeff's apartment when the unmistakable whine of a Ferrari engine alerted us to D.H.'s arrival.

The Ferrari, shiny red and with the top off, pulled in smoothly to the curb with D.H. behind the wheel smiling up at us with bright white teeth.

"Hi gorgeous! It's been too long!"

"I know," Rosalynd said, and leaned into the car since D.H. had remained behind the wheel and gave him a hug and a peck on the cheek. D.H. was younger than I expected, only a few years older than I was if I wasn't mistaken. Rosalynd then introduced Jeff and me.

D.H. shook hands with us and we exchanged greetings and pleasantries for a couple of minutes, but it wasn't too long before he was looking at his watch. "I'd love to stay and chat, but I have this package to deliver," he grinned mischievously, pointing at a large basket of goodies with wine, wrapped in pink cellophane and topped with a bright red bow propped in the passenger seat next to him that none of us could have possibly overlooked, and went on, "and I'm a little pressed for time, so if you don't have any objections, Chris, I thought we could talk on the way."

That was fine with me, so after getting a thumbs up for luck from Jeff and a hug from Rosalynd, I hopped in next to D.H., maneuvering the basket of goodies out of the seat first and onto my lap, since there was nowhere else in the car for it, and had barely leaned back when D.H. gunned the accelerator and the Ferrari leaped back onto the road.

We were headed out of the Valley again up into the Mayacamas Range, where D.H. was delivering the frilly package, this time not up Spring Mountain but farther south on the Oakville Grade, which cut its way through the northern part of the Mt. Veeder appellation. Only about ten percent of the appellation was currently under vines, with the rest mostly a tangle of redwood, madrone, laurel, and various kinds of oak. The Oakville Grade was steep and narrow in places, curving back and forth upon itself as it climbed, but the horsepower under the Ferrari's hood was more than up to the task.

D.H. raced eagerly into the curves and then accelerated even faster out of them, and feeling a bit shy of speed since my wreck, I had to shut my eyes and hold on tightly to the basket of goodies and remind myself to take deep breaths, which wasn't difficult with the top down. It was no wonder, moments later D.H. asked if something was wrong.

"No," I said, bracing my feet against the floorboards as we took another turn and wondering how all four wheels had stayed on the ground. "I just didn't know you were an Indy car driver."

D.H. smiled with his teeth, "I did own an Indy car!" And then as if expecting me to doubt him went on, "Yeah, I did! I really did!" But I didn't doubt him, because for one thing, we hadn't slowed down. "Actually I had two Indy cars! Traveled with 'em all over the country. Of course that was years ago."

"So, who's this basket for?" I asked trying to get my mind on another subject.

"My girlfriend!" D.H. grinned.

"I had guessed as much," I said, "the pink wrapping sort of tipped me off."

"Yeah, she's a little mad at me at the moment. She thinks our relationship has progressed to the stage that we should be living together. Either I move in with her — which would be impossible, or she moves in with me — which would be preposterous!"

I smiled. "Why, what's wrong with that?"

"Don't get me wrong, she's gorgeous, but I once lived with six girls in the same apartment, so never again." Then as if I doubted him, "Oh, yeah! Yeah, six! At the same time! In a beach house in So. Cal!" He shook his head, remembering, "If I see one more pair of pantyhose hanging from the shower, I'll used them to hang myself."

I laughed.

D.H. then got a buzz on his cell and fished it out of his pocket with one hand, while taking a hairpin turn with the other. Glancing at the number on his cell, he said to me, "Oh, gotta take this," and answered. "General—"

After a few minutes hearing only one side of the conversation, I managed to piece together that a high ranking general in the Air Force — the person on the other end of the call — recently had been given a party in his honor and D.H. had delivered 'above and beyond the call of duty,' and the general was appreciative. They talked on about when the general could come out and visit the wine country and D.H. would make certain that they — the general and his wife — would have a wonderful time, and the general was going to take him up on it, when D.H. finally hung up.

"General Brickton — a member of the Joint Chiefs of Staff," he said explaining.

My eyebrows went up.

"Yeah, I had to take that one," he said, putting the cell back in his front pocket. "You don't keep a general waiting."

I asked him then about his various businesses and learned D.H. Hackett Industries was currently into distribution, real estate, and radio, not to mention a number of web-based projects. I wondered how he had time to sleep let alone keep so many businesses moving forward at the same time. 'Can you hack it?' indeed.

D.H. sailed through another tight turn, but had to downshift abruptly upon seeing on the road ahead a long line of idling cars stopped bumper to bumper. There was no place to go around, the roadway being too narrow, so we had to slow down and stop behind them. He glanced again at his watch, "Now what?"

Before I could venture a guess, he was out of the Ferrari and striding down the road, passing the idling cars to see what the trouble was. Seemed sensible that I stay in the car with the basket, so I did. Moments later, D.H. returned.

"Road kill. Somebody hit a deer." And he proceeded to the trunk of the Ferrari, which was the size of a lunch box and retrieved a large knife, just like the ones braves used in the movies to scalp people with. D.H. then started back down the row of cars, saying to me as he went, "I'll be right back."

And he was. He hadn't been gone three minutes when here he came, in one hand the large knife, and in the other — about eight inches of just severed deer hoof. He didn't say anything, or even glance at me, but headed instead to the trunk again and carefully put the knife and bloody deer hoof in a bag, and then put the bag into the trunk and shut it. He then climbed back behind the wheel, and seconds later the traffic began to clear and we continued on.

What had just happened? What could D.H. possibly need with a deer hoof? I hadn't a clue. Was he a serial killer or what? I didn't know if I should ask him about it or not, and clearly he wasn't volunteering anything. So we rode along together quietly, if you call the roar of a Ferrari engine quiet, when after a bit D.H. broke the silence by asking me about Vic. So I set aside any questions I had and filled him in on what had happened at Maverick Cellars with Vic and some of the other things that had happened and he seemed well informed already about most of it — like everybody seemed to be in the Valley these days. I then filled him in on the white pickup that had been following me, and about being forced off the road. And hearing that, D.H. glanced urgently in his rearview mirror, before smiling at me and saying, "Don't worry. Nobody's back there!"

Before I could go on, his cell phone interrupted, buzzing in his pocket again, and D.H. fished it out and looked at the number. "Oh, gotta take this one," and then said, "Hello?"

This call took longer to finish and was more elaborate, but from what I could get from my end, D.H. was confirming the visit in a few weeks of some very important people coming into the Napa Valley from the East Coast — times schedules, itineraries, plane arrivals and departures were being carefully covered. When D.H. finally hung up, he turned to me and said, "That was John Villardos — the billionaire. Worth $2.6 billion!"

"Had to take the call," I said.

"Had to," D.H. echoed, replacing the phone and then asking what he could do for me. After fielding favors for first a general and then a billionaire, I was a bit hesitant, but plunged in anyway and told D.H. about wanting to get ahold of Gerry Zacks, and Gerry being incommunicado and then how I had been blocked at his place of business, and finally about our idea of maybe getting at somebody close to Gerry who might be willing to help us.

"Yeah, I know Gerry!" D.H. had said, when I first started, and when I finished, he fished for the cell in his pocket again and said, "No problem. Let me make a call." Driving with one hand he thumbed the scroll button on his phone with his other, searching his directory until he found the number he was after and put in the call. He must've had a lot of practice driving that way, because he hardly strayed from the road. "Sarah McCauley? D.H. Hackett!" He then laughed and grinned at me as if I had heard how she had just responded, so I smiled back. I listened for awhile on this end and heard them exchange some ribald banter that I didn't exactly follow before D.H. got on to why he was calling. "A friend of mine, Chris Garrett, a winemaker here in Napa, yeah — I'd appreciate it if he could stop by tomorrow, uh-huh, and have a short chat with you. He's well — I'll let Chris fill you in on what he wants to chat about. Tomorrow? Great, I appreciate this, Sarah! Thanks for your help. Okay. Bye!"

D.H. then smiled at me and said, "You've got a meeting tomorrow at FuTel, with the V.P. of Marketing, Sarah McCauley. The rest is up to you." His smile turned mischievous. "Sarah — now there's a girl that oughta be asking me to move in with her!"

We had reached his current girlfriend's house and turned into the drive. The overgrowth along the side of the drive was thick and it wasn't until we reached the house that I could see how high we had come up the mountain. Through an opening in the trees — beyond the house, which was fashioned cleverly to look like a Swiss chalet — was an eagle-eyed view of Napa Valley stretching into the distance below.

"Nice view," I said.

D.H. stopped the car and got out. A green Miata could be glimpsed parked in a garage that stood apart from the house, so apparently somebody was home. I handed the basket of goodies to D.H. and he took a deep breath.

"You think she'll take you back?" I asked.

D.H. flashed me a winning smile, and said, "How could she resist?" and then headed confidently up the walk and up to the front door.

I watched from the Ferrari wondering how his girlfriend was going to take the peace offering, when D.H. having finally reached the door, carefully set the basket down, reached for the bell, rang it — and then took off running!

He was cackling with hilarity as he raced back along the walk, nearly tripping on some flowers that skirted the edge and then reached the car and hopped in. In moments the Ferrari was in gear, and with the engine racing we peeled out in the gravel and sped back down the drive.

The next day, around five to eleven, Jeff and I were standing in front of Future Telecom, Inc., south of Market in San Francisco, looking up at an old though recently renovated building. Rosalynd having driven us into the City had dropped us off and then had gone on to take care of some errands having to do with her mother's charity work that she was also helping with and had had to put on hold the last couple of days on account of my car wreck and subsequent convalescence. We had agreed to meet up afterward downtown for lunch near the Ferry Building.

Heading inside FuTel, Jeff and I glanced around and not seeing Gerry Zacks anywhere at hand, turned toward the reception desk on the right situated directly across from a bank of elevators. It wasn't until we were nearly to the desk and up to the woman behind it that I finally recognized who she was.

Jeff, also recognizing her, jokingly made a noise like a horse blowing, which caused the woman who was busy at a computer monitor to jerk her head up.

It was Bridget Bordeaux.

Her eyes leaped toward Jeff first, but then when they finally focused on me, she blurted, "Oh, God!" and quickly hid her face in her hands.

Jeff was grinning so big I had to elbow him.

"Ms. Monroe," I queried, trying not to sound flustered myself. "I see you remember me."

"Oh, God," she repeated, but she was also now peeking at us through her fingers. "I'm so embarrassed."

"We had no idea you worked here," I said, smiling in spite of every effort not to. "We have – or rather I have an appointment with Sarah McCauley at eleven."

Ms. Monroe, her face burning a deep red, quickly looked through her appointment ledger and found my meeting with Sarah at eleven as arranged by D.H. "Yes, it's here. Take the left elevator to the top floor and ask for Sarah. She's in Marketing."

I nodded, and then asked, "You're not the person who answers the phone around here?" remembering the female voice that earlier had given me the runaround.

"Not usually," Ms. Monroe said. "I'm filling in for a girl, just for today." She was glancing at Jeff again, his big grin getting her to even smile a little. Then suddenly giggling, she shooed us away. "Now, go to your meeting!"

As Jeff and I headed as ordered for the left elevator, he glanced back once and then said to me, "You know, she's very cute."

I took a big breath, just as the elevator doors opened and said, "You have no idea."

Which of course made him laugh.

Gerry Zacks wasn't in the elevator with us as we rose smoothly to the top floor, nor was he in the hallway when we stepped out, but Sarah McCauley was. Her office was down a few doors from the elevators and she was there waiting for us, Ms. Monroe having most likely given her the heads up on our arrival while we rode up.

"Chris Garrett?" she enquired.

202

"That's me," I said, and approaching, took her outstretched hand.

"Sarah," she returned, informal and friendly, though I did see her eyes dart once quickly toward Jeff.

In fairness she had been expecting only me, not Jeff and me, so I quickly explained, "I brought a friend along. Jeff Beckwell. Hope you don't mind."

"Mind? Why should I mind? You're on time. It's eleven on the dot. I appreciate people who can be punctual." Sarah was all smiles, but as she shook Jeff's hand in greeting she carefully asked him, "Are you in the wine business as well?"

"No. Law enforcement."

"Oh. I see."

The V.P. of Marketing at FuTel had a window office and Jeff and I took in the fantastic view Sarah had of San Francisco Bay with the Bay Bridge jutting out across it — and if you craned your neck and looked down and to the left, you could just made out Giants Stadium and McCovey Cove, which I pointed out to Jeff, who nodded.

Sarah motioned us toward a knee high table in front of the window already placed with two chairs, and Jeff thinking fast grabbed one near her desk making it three, so each of us sat down and got comfortable, though I didn't know how comfortable Ms. McCauley was the way she had fastened her teeth firmly on her lower lip. She was still eyeing Jeff. "So is this official?"

"Well," I said, interrupting, "if you mean, did the Napa Valley Sheriff's office send us — no."

"I see." Her eyes looked back at me and held steady for a moment. "Listen, when D.H. called and told me your name, I'll admit I recognized it. I read the newspapers. I figured you were coming to chat about Victor Miranda's death."

"Actually what we want—" I started, but Sarah stopped me with a raised palm.

"You'll want to know if I knew Vic. I knew him, not socially. He was here a number of times, with Gerry. It's been awhile since I last saw him — six months, maybe a year. I'm afraid, I can't be much more help than that."

"What I meant to say," I said, trying again, "it's not Victor Miranda we came to talk to you about."

"Oh?"

"Not directly," Jeff added.

"Oh. I see."

"We've been trying to contact Gerry Zacks." So I told her about my troubles trying to track him down.

She nodded sympathetically, "Sometimes Gerry can be difficult to reach."

"Don't I know it," I said, nodding.

Her eyes held steady on me again. "I'll be honest with you, since D.H. asked me to help you. But since this isn't official, I don't want a word of this getting out."

Jeff and I both nodded.

"Gerry isn't here."

"Where is he?" I asked.

"That's the point. No one knows. He hasn't been in the office for over two weeks. That's why the runaround on the phone. We don't want news of his absence leaking out."

Jeff asked, "Why not?"

Sarah leaned back in her chair. "It's not that Gerry hasn't done this before. A few years ago, when the tech bubble burst, Gerry was gone for nearly five months." She went on, "Yeah, nobody knew where he'd gone until he returned. Seems he was in Mongolia. The Buryat Republic, can you believe it? Living in grass huts and drinking horse blood with the natives — while also helping them get web access using satellites. Sometimes Gerry can be a bit eccentric."

"No doubt," I said. "And if word got out he was on another self-imposed sabbatical—"

"That's right," she agreed. "Not something we want broadcasted. Future Telecom can ill afford more idle gossip."

"You mean, gossip about your financial troubles?" Jeff offered.

"That's just type of talk we want to avoid," Sarah said, reacting strongly. "As a matter of fact, Future Telecom is currently up this quarter above Wall Street expectations, and forecasts predict a healthy year's end, so no, we don't want news of Gerry's absence negatively influencing stockholder confidence in Future Telecom. We believe the future of telecommunications remains bright, just like our name." Well, she was the V.P. of Marketing after all.

Jeff and I rode back down the elevator more informed, but no closer to locating Gerry, and if Gerry was off drinking horse blood again somewhere on the Russian Steppes, then we'd certainly play hell trying to find him. Another dead end.

When the elevator doors opened, we headed for the exit, but Ms. Monroe still behind the reception desk was beckoning to us, so we made a detour.

As we joined her, she said under her breath, "I know why you're here. It's on account of Victor, isn't it?"

"Mostly," I said. "We're also trying to find your boss Gerry Zacks."

"He's not here."

"Yeah, we heard."

"Does Gerry know something about Victor's murder?"

"He might," I offered.

Jeff put his hand out, smiling, "I'm Jeff, by the way."

Ms. Monroe took his hand, but her smile remained wary, "Pleasure to meet you."

"The pleasure's mine," Jeff said, still grinning — the cad — which got her to thaw a bit. He then said, "Do you happen to know where Gerry is?"

"No." Ms. Monroe was still keeping her voice down. "But if I had to guess, I'd say he was out climbing rocks. It's his latest obsession. Did you see the climbing wall set up at the back?"

We both shook our heads.

"Must be thirty feet tall — with all these handholds attached on it. Makes me dizzy just looking up at it."

"Rock-climbing, huh?" Jeff confirmed.

"That's right. If I wanted to find Gerry, that's the first place I'd look."

Chapter 17

WHEN WE GOT back to the Valley, Jeff needed to talk with his colleagues at the Sheriff's Department and see what progress was being made locating the white pickup, and also to see if there was any interest in locating Gerry Zacks. That left Rosalynd and me on our own, and I still had an urgent need to check on my wine at Maverick Cellars. I had put off visiting the winery for far too long as it was, and Rosalynd decided to come along with me.

It was just after closing time, and there was little activity inside. The destemmer-crusher was standing quiet, and the floor was washed and hoses were hanging in their proper places, and the crush pad looked tidy, which made me smile. So far, so good, I was thinking, when Rosalynd and I heard voices and then raucous laughter coming from the winery's kitchen. We headed that way.

A card game was in progress. Álvaro and Henri were at the big table with a number of Latino co-workers playing quarter-a-hand poker and letting off steam. Cans of Modelo and limes were scattered amongst the cards and the money. When we stepped in, Henri saw us first. "Voila! You're just in time!"

All heads turned our way and Rosalynd and I had the floor. Álvaro spun in his chair and shook my hand vigorously once I had reached the table. "Bring any money, jefe?" he asked slyly.

"No. I'm just here to check the wine," I explained and then introduced Rosalynd to the troops. There were more handshakes all around.

Henri said, "We were told you wouldn't be back until next week!"

I shrugged, modestly.

"Speaking of wine," Álvaro said, sounding suddenly awkward. "You know the fruit you and Tony set aside?"

"Yeah," I answered carefully. "What happened to it?"

"Well, Eric saw it. He liked it. So now he is making his own wine from it."

"Oh, he is?" I had had the feeling something like this might happen. It was a let down, to be sure, but what could I do about it?

Álvaro could read the disappointment in my face. "Sorry, jefe."

I waved it away. "Forget it."

The card game resumed. Álvaro asked a young woman seated across from him named Gisela if she was playing this hand, and when she grimaced and stuck her tongue out at him, he snickered.

"What, Gisela's losing?" I asked, which set everybody laughing.

Álvaro clarified, "She has lost fifty-three straight hands."

"Ouch."

He went on, "We felt sorry for her. So we gave her a pair to start, but no good. Then a three of a kind." He snickered, "Still she can not win."

One of the cellar workers said, "No ella necesita una limpia con huevos de gallina."

Álvaro quickly retorted, "No ella necesita una limpia pero con huevos de avestruz," which caused the whole table to erupt in laughter. Gisela's eyes flashed dangerously at Álvaro, but he was laughing too hard to take the warning seriously.

Rosalynd, not following the exchange, asked, "What did he say?" So I told her that Gisela needed to clean herself with a chicken egg to ward off her bad luck, and Álvaro had retorted, with her luck she'd need to use an ostrich egg. Rosalynd smiled at the joke, but she was also eyeing me closely. "I didn't know you spoke Spanish."

I shrugged modestly. "I've picked up a little, here and there. Comes in handy sometimes."

We watched a few more hands being played, and then I asked Álvaro if Eric was around.

"No, he split around three." He motioned at the card players around the table. "We are the only ones here."

I nodded and with Rosalynd we begged off and left them to their game.

First I wanted to check the tanks currently going through fermentation and quickly saw that I needn't have bothered. Álvaro had everything in order. I looked over the logbooks anyway and charted the progress the wines were currently making, even Eric's, which from the logs I could see that Álvaro was doing most of the pump-overs and seeing to the nutrients. Maybe the cuvée would be fine after all, I thought, if Eric was leaving all the winemaking up to Álvaro.

Rosalynd showed an interest in everything that went into making wine, which of course inflated my head like a balloon, and I soon was blabbing on about fermentation temperatures and choice of yeasts — wild or cultivated — and about the nearly infinite number of processes and variables and techniques — voodoo or otherwise — that we had to choose from that could positively affect the finished wines.

Suddenly conscious of all my blabbing, I said, "Sorry, I get carried away."

"Are you kidding?" Rosalynd said smiling. "I'm totally fascinated." Her eyes were very bright with that hint of amusement in them. "And I like all the talk about wine too."

"You do?" I said, smiling back.

"Uh-huh."

"Then, shall we check out the caves?"

"I'd like that very much," Rosalynd said.

The caves stretched back under the hillside behind the

winery and kept the wines once barreled down at a cool and constant temperature, varying little whether in the heat of summer or the cold of winter. Once inside, I flipped on the lights and we could see the barrels stacked two high lining both sides of the cave.

As Rosalynd fingered delicately at the cobweb-like mold growing over the walls and across the ceiling, I grabbed a wine thief and a couple of glasses from a table just inside the cave entrance and said, "How about a tour?"

Rosalynd's eyes sparkled in the muted light of the cave, and she nodded, and taking my arm, we strolled between the stacked barrels and past branching tunnels also lined with more barrels and winemaking equipment. Rosalynd marveled, "How far back into the mountain does this go?"

"Oh, quite a ways. You'd be surprised. There's over half a mile of caves branching off in various directions."

"Really?" She took this in while looking around. Then she noticed the pipes lining the cave walls and asked, "What's this for?"

"Water lines. We use a lot of water making wine." I then pointed at the pressurized tanks. "This is argon. We use it to blanket the surface of wine in tanks and barrels since it's heavier than air. Keeps the oxygen at bay."

"What about this other tank?"

"That's SO_2. Sulfur-dioxide gas. We fill empty barrels with it to preserve the sweetness and keep mold and other harmful stuff from growing inside. It's very acrid smelling, like burnt matchsticks."

Rosalynd nodded.

We had reached the place I wanted to check, barrels going through secondary fermentation, which was a process that softened the acidity of the wines and also helped them taste more supple and complex. I lifted a bung from one of the barrels and took a sniff inside. The smell prickled my nose from the carbon dioxide blowing off yet also had a subtle aroma of berry jam. I put my ear down to listen. Gentle burbles from the gases coming off the wine told me the fermentation was still going on. I smiled at Rosalynd and had her do the same.

"Do you hear the wine? It's talking to you. Whispering—"

She smiled at the gentle burbling. "What is it whispering?"

"Yummy, very yummy, very beautiful. And the wine is pretty good too."

Rosalynd's eyes twinkled at me.

I grinned. "Shall we continue?"

"Uh-huh." And she took her ear away from the wine, but before I could replace the bung, she took one more sniff. "It smells very inviting."

"And it'll just get better, believe me."

"I believe you."

We then moved past a long line of empty barrels stacked five high waiting to be filled. I showed Rosalynd how if you stacked them up correctly the barrels would nest into one another, without falling.

"Nest — I like that. So reassuring, like coming home."

She had that amused look of hers going again. I decided

to continue the tour farther back into the cave where barrels of wine were being laid down to age. I explained, "The French have a term for this stage of winemaking — élevage."

Rosalynd, recognizing the word, said, "To lift?"

"Yeah, almost." I nodded and set down the glasses and wine thief I'd been holding to have at a nearby barrel bung. "Actually, to raise, like in raising or rearing a child."

"How expressive. I never knew winemakers had such — sensitivity," she said, gently teasing.

She was standing close to me, looking up into my eyes with a corner of her lip curled in amusement, and if for nothing else than to remove that silly grin, I bent down and kissed her.

She didn't push away, but moved in closer, and wrapping our arms around each other, the kiss lingered on and on and could've lingered on and on indefinitely in my opinion if we didn't have to eventually come up for air. When we finally did, I noticed she still had that silly grin of hers going. Maybe it was permanent.

Breathing halfway normal again, I said, "I blame that on the wine."

"But we haven't had any wine."

"Oh — then we better have some!"

"Okay."

Rosalynd's eyes sure sparkled in that cave light. I handed her the glasses and got out the thief and removing the bung from the barrel pulled out some wine and dribbled a little into each glass. Then I returned the bung to the barrel, and accepted one of the glasses from Rosalynd.

We both swirled the wine around in the glass and then held it to our nose and smelled it before tasting. The wine which was still a little closed in my opinion, needed a few more months in barrel to really open up, but to be honest, neither of us were thinking all that much about the wine. I watched her take a sip and swallow, and then run her tongue over her lips, all the while watching me over the rim of her glass. I wanted to kiss her again and I did, and it was even better than the first time. Linking our arms we strolled on through the rest of the cave carrying our glasses, moving past the aging barrels until coming to a section of tunnel that wasn't being used as of yet. Empty barrels stacked two abreast in stainless steel barrel racks had been placed before the tunnel opening, blocking the way, so I handed her my glass, and went back a short ways and scrounged up a pallet jack.

Rosalynd peered down the passage, which was very dark, the lights not having been turned on in this section. I got the jack under the barrel racks and hoisted them up and rolled them aside. Then I flipped on the lights, a switch being on the wall at the left, and the tunnel sprang suddenly into view. We continued our tour.

But it wasn't too much farther that we came to the end of the cave about as far back as possible into the hillside, upon which the tunnel branched. Turning the corner we butted up against what looked like thousands of cases of wine stacked on pallets, which was news to me. I didn't know anything was being stored this far back in the cave and said so to Rosalynd.

"Maybe they moved them in while you were absent," she offered.

"Maybe," I said, but looking closer at the stacks, I saw that the cases of wine were Maverick Cellars' Reserve bottling, and there was a hell of a lot of it back here — it was just a guess, but I'd say our whole release.

I must've looked confused, because Rosalynd asked, "What is it?"

I pulled at the shrink-wrap binding the cases on the pallets and got one of the boxes open and pulled out a bottle. I held it out so we could both see it. Yep, it was the Reserve all right. "This isn't right."

"What do you mean?" Rosalynd set our glasses aside, and took a closer look at the bottle I was holding.

"I mean this wine shouldn't be here. It should've been shipped already. It's all allocated, anyway."

"Allocated?"

"Already sold to customers. As far as I know, we've already sent this wine to them — over a month ago."

"Then why is it still here?"

I shook my head, still looking intently down at the bottle I was holding, when it hit me. "I think this is a clue!"

"A clue — into Vic's murder?"

"Yep. This wine is a forgery."

I looked up at Rosalynd to see her reaction and as our eyes met, everything went black. Not because I had been hit on the head again, but because somebody had just turned out the lights. Rosalynd made a short little shriek and her hands groped at me in the complete darkness, which you can't blame her for. I wanted to shriek myself, because I knew with growing certainty that we were not alone. There was somebody else in the cave!

I found Rosalynd's hand in the darkness and gave it a comforting squeeze, or what I hoped was comforting, but because my heart was racing as much as hers was I wasn't sure I didn't squeeze a little too hard. You haven't experienced complete darkness until you're literally buried under a mountain. Saying it's unnerving isn't telling the whole truth. I pulled Rosalynd close and finding her ear in the darkness whispered, "Are you all right?"

"Yes." Her voice broke a little.

"If I lead, can you follow?"

"Yes." She sounded better that time.

"We need to get out of here. Those lights didn't turn off by accident."

"I know." Rosalynd then asked, still whispering, "Is there only one way out?"

"No. There's another exit around the hill. We'll try that one first."

"But we can't see."

I squeezed her hand again. "Don't worry. I know the way."

So I began leading Rosalynd toward the other exit, moving slowly so we didn't bang into anything. I had to keep my bearing, because all the different tunnels made it a maze, and if I guessed wrong and turned down the wrong passage – I'd just have to keep it straight.

It was slow going, and when I found an obstacle in our path, like a barrel or piece of equipment, I eased Rosalynd carefully forward until she too could feel it for herself and avoid injury, then we would continue on. We were making steady progress and had reached the section of the cave where the nesting barrels were stacked. It wasn't too much farther to the exit, and I was just about to whisper this to Rosalynd, when a sharp bang just like a wooden bat hitting a baseball rang out loudly directly before us, followed by the hollow rumbling of tumbling barrels.

I yanked Rosalynd backward and turned my back on the rumbling to protect her, knowing full well what was happening — somebody had just knocked loose one of the barrel blocks bracing the nesting barrels, bringing the whole stack down. The first empty barrel hit me high on the shoulder driving me forward. Colliding with Rosalynd, I stumbled and she fell as another shriek escaped her throat, and I fell on top of her. That was when the second barrel slammed me sharply in the thigh and then the barrels came so fast it was the fifth and sixth barrel that was clobbering me. I tucked Rosalynd under my chest as the barrels tumbled over our heads. And then the rumbling and rolling was past and the silence descended over us again.

Rosalynd was breathing hard so I knew she was alive, and so was I, but a couple of those barrels had caught me where it hurts and for a couple of seconds I didn't move. My left leg felt numb. Then I found her ear in the dark. "Hurt?"

DAVID G. WHITE

"No."

"Can you move?"

"Yes."

"We'll go back. Try the other exit." There were too many barrels lying around us now to go forward anyway.

So we got carefully to our feet, our ears keen for any sound ahead or behind for that matter, but whoever had brought those barrels down had most likely stepped back out of the way and was too far back now to be heard, and anyhow I suspected he was wasting no time hustling around to block the other exit.

I rubbed at my thigh where the barrel had clobbered me good, which helped the tingling and numbness some so I could put weight on it, and taking Rosalynd's hand, we began edging around the loose barrels in our path.

I needed a plan. We couldn't wander around in the darkness forever. We would need to try getting past that exit eventually, if we ever expected to get out of here, but what to do about the bastard that was waiting to waylay us? Then I had it.

As we groped our way in the darkness, I was also feeling for something that might help, and it wasn't a stick or club to do battle with, it was something better. I nearly kicked it before I found it, which would've been a disaster. I bent down and lifted it by the handle and it made a tiny metal creak.

Rosalynd whispered at me, "What're you doing?"

"I've got an idea." I sidled up to the cave wall between the barrels and found a water spigot, and turned it carefully on.

Water poured forth into my bucket, ringing against the metal like Niagara Falls. A thousand Niagara Falls! When I finally had it filled and the spigot turned off, the silence was even louder. I groped quickly for the hose that I knew was coiled up and hanging on the pressurized tank nearby and found it. I plunged the end of the hose into the water.

Rosalynd whispered, "I think I heard somebody."

"Just a few seconds more," and I found the stopcock on the tank that was connected to the hose I had just placed in the water and turned it. A hiss of bubbles erupted in the bucket of water, along with a faint acrid odor. I let the bubbles continue for a moment longer and then turned off the gas and removed the hose.

Rosalynd was at my ear. "He's right over there!"

I had also heard the scrape of probably his shoe against the floor. He was eager and was coming for us, and taking Rosalynd's hand, I pulled her gently along the opposite wall, inching our way closer and closer to the exit I knew was now only about twenty or thirty feet from us, trying not to make a sound or even breathe for fear of revealing our exact location, when a flashlight clicked on about twelve feet away and had us in its beam. Not waiting, I swung the bucket of water and splashed the full amount directly at the light. The gas held by the water instantly released like a noxious cloud, engulfing whoever was holding the light in suffocating sulfurous fumes. I then hurled the metal bucket, but I don't know if I hit my target, because I had already taken Rosalynd's hand and was racing toward the exit.

Behind us, amidst the rattling sounds of the bouncing bucket, I heard first the stumble of footsteps in pursuit and then a desperate gasp and horrendous choking, and then I was at the door fumbling at the latch, hoping it hadn't been locked from the outside, when all at once the door sprang open and we were out.

Light spilled into the cave and looking back I expected to see the identity of our assailant, but all that was there was the metal bucket rocking back and forth, and the slick of sulfur water. I ran back inside over Rosalynd's protests and looked down the first branching tunnel, but it was too dark to see anything, and by the time I got to the lights and had them on, whoever it was had made his escape out the other exit.

Rosalynd ran to me as I left the cave again, and throwing her arms around my neck, buried her face against my chest. She was trembling, and I patted her gently on the back. Both of us were breathing hard from the exertion, when I caught the acrid whiff of sulfur emanating from the cave. We stepped farther away into the fresh air, and that was how Álvaro with the others from the card game having rushed from the kitchen found us.

"We heard yelling!" Álvaro said with alarm.

I was still holding Rosalynd, "Somebody in the cave nearly did us in with another accident."

The troops reacted with disbelief and anger.

"He escaped out the other exit," I explained. "We didn't see who it was."

"Just now?" Álvaro asked.

I nodded.

"Perhaps if we hurry," Henri was all set for the chase.

"No, he's long gone now. Don't worry, we'll catch 'em."

"You are bleeding, jefe!" Álvaro pointed at my arm.

My shirt had been ripped at the sleeve and underneath — most likely from one of the tumbling barrels — a patch of skin had been sufficiently abraded. I hadn't even felt it.

Álvaro pointed at my head. "And you lost your bandage."

I reached up and felt the exposed stitches above my brow. "I must look like I belong in a Frankenstein movie."

Rosalynd was concerned over my wounds and started examining them, and I noticed the front of her clothes were dusty from our tumble in the cave and both her hands were scuffed.

"You okay?"

"Yes," she nodded. "I'm all right now. But my heart's still racing a thousand miles an hour."

"Yeah, I often have that effect on women," I said, which got her to smile.

Álvaro asked, "Who do you think it was?"

"I don't know. It was too dark to see, but I know one thing, he's connected with Maverick Cellars," which hit the troops close to home and they reacted with more disbelief. It also reminded me of something. "I'll be right back."

I left Rosalynd with the others and sprinted again into the cave, heading clear back to where the suspected wine cases were stacked and hustled back out moments later with two of the Reserve bottles.

Álvaro glanced at the bottles, but said he didn't know anything had been stored that far back in the cave. "No reason to go back there."

I nodded. "If I hadn't been giving Rosalynd a tour, I never would have known about it myself. Why would anybody suspect there was anything back there? For all I know that wine could've been stored there for awhile."

"Who at Maverick Cellars could've been party to this?" Rosalynd asked.

I shrugged. "Eric, maybe?"

Álvaro asked, "Whoever did this, you think they also killed Vic and then tried to run you off the road?"

"Yeah," I said.

"Then it could not be Eric. He was crushing fruit with us the whole time when you had your crash."

Before I could absorb what this meant, Jeff roared up next to the crush pad in his Jeep. Rosalynd and I walked over to him, and the troops followed as Jeff killed the ignition.

I asked, "Did you see who it was?"

Jeff remained seated, and I saw how he was glancing up and down at Rosalynd and me, noticing our worse-for-wear appearance, so I filled him in on what had just happened in the cave, and I saw him set his jaw.

"Yeah, I saw him," he finally said, looking grim.

Rosalynd blurted, "You saw him! How?"

Jeff smiled, but there was no warmth in it. "I've been watching you two from a distance, ever since getting back from the City."

As Rosalynd took this in, she shot me a questioning look, and I shrugged. I knew all about what Jeff was doing.

"So who was it?" I asked him again.

"Matt Bakerwood."

Chapter
18

JEFF STARTED UP the Jeep and I went around to the passenger door to get in, when Rosalynd interrupted us. "Are you going over there? Right now?"

"Yep," I said. "Time we had a chat with Matt Bakerwood."

"Then I'm going with you," she said, setting her jaw much like Jeff had done, and followed me around the Jeep. I had her sit in the front with him. I climbed in back.

Álvaro said, "I will go too." And he hopped into the back seat with me, while Henri and some of the others voiced their desire to follow us in another vehicle, but I told them about my concern that nobody be allowed to mess with the cases of wine still in the caves, and Henri nodded and said he'd stay with the others and watch over them. With that taken care of, Jeff shoved the Jeep in gear and off we went.

It only took a few minutes to get to Bakerwood Winery, and pulling into the front entrance, it was easy to see that Matt's truck wasn't in the parking lot, so I told Jeff to drive around to the other side of the property where some storage buildings were located with a number of sheds used to park vineyard equipment to see if he was there.

Once on the other side, we turned onto the service road that ran behind the equipment sheds and I happened to glance inside the last shed furthest from the paved road and saw something that caused my pulse to race. "Hold it!"

Jeff hit the brakes. I hopped out of the Jeep and as I headed over to the shed I heard everybody clamber out to follow. The equipment shed had a metal slider, but it was slightly ajar, and I thought I had caught a glimpse of something white through the crack. I peeked in, and then having satisfied myself, rolled the door back so the others could see what I had found.

It was the white pickup.

It was Matt Bakerwood's ranch truck to be exact. I knew I had seen it before. I just hadn't placed it. I went around to the front and looked at the bumper. I saw clearly that on the side that had collided with my pickup it was still bent back against the frame.

Jeff was looking at the license plate, or rather where the license plate should have been, only the pickup didn't have one. "The Sheriff's Department would've played hell running down this vehicle, without plates." He looked up at us. "More than likely it hasn't been registered in years."

"It's used only around the vineyard," I explained, "never on legal roads."

Jeff said, "Only we know that's not true."

We were interrupted in our examination when we heard vehicles approaching, tires crunching gravel along with the throaty rumbling of a large diesel. Stepping out of the shed, I saw Matt coming towards us in another pickup, much newer, and riding with him in the back bed were a number of his cellar crew. Behind Matt's pickup was a large flatbed diesel — not loaded — and driven by Halleran. It wasn't hard to guess where Matt and his cellar crew were headed in such a hurry and what they might be intending to load onto the flatbed once they got there. Only Jeff's Jeep was blocking the road ahead of them.

We stepped from the shed and walked out onto the road to meet them, and Matt, only at the last instant, whipped his pickup into an aggressive slide and came to a halt. Halleran stopped the big diesel behind the pickup and set the air brake, which whooshed sharply. The cellar crew piled out of Matt's pickup, and Matt threw open his door angrily and started toward us. Counting Matt and Halleran there were eleven of them. The way Matt was leaning into it I thought I'd better get in the first poke, or rather, the first word.

"Where you going, Matt?"

"Get out of the way, Chris!" He pointed at Jeff's Jeep. "Move the rig!"

"We just want to talk with you," I said, trying to keep my

voice level.

"Yeah, well, maybe I don't want to talk, so move the Jeep, and then get the hell off my property!" He stopped about ten feet away, his eyes very wide taking us in, his feet and legs fidgeting nervously. "Unless you want to be tossed out on your ass!"

The cellar crew mostly Latino was also coming towards us and fanning out belligerently, and the way they moved, I knew they meant business. Rosalynd was at my side, and I put her behind me. Álvaro was a bit farther to my right, but he was standing his ground, and Jeff, his eyes watching Matt lazily, swaggered towards him regardless of the hostility of the cellar crew. His shoulders hung loose, leaving his arms to dangle carelessly at his sides.

"We know it was you," Jeff said, his voice pitched lower than usual.

Matt, still fidgety, was now eyeing Jeff. "I don't give a shit what you know or don't know. You're trespassing!"

One of the crewmembers, a burly looking Mexican about three inches taller and a healthy forty pounds heavier than Jeff, wearing a ball cap stepped between him and Matt. From his pocket he pulled out a large knife, even bigger than the one D.H. had had in his Ferrari.

Matt smirked. "If you want to fight, don't think Jorge won't use it. Right, bro?"

Jorge just flashed at us his gold-capped teeth.

Matt then laughed, and Halleran joined him. I never liked Halleran much. Matt, still fidgeting, pressed his advantage and said, "Hey, Álvaro, you here too? How many names you actually got, anyway? Ten?"

Álvaro took a step forward, and Matt's eyes widened even more at him.

"Watch it, homeboy. You don't wanna get stuck by Jorge."

Álvaro stopped when a few of the other crewmembers circled closer to corral him in.

Matt went on nastily, "You know why your mamma gave you so many names — 'cause she couldn't make up her mind who was your papa!" and he hooted loudly while Halleran and the rest of the cellar crew chuckled along.

Jeff then started forward again, which caused Matt to stop hooting and Jorge to stop flashing his capped teeth. But Jeff wasn't stopping, and for that matter neither was Jorge backing up, and I felt Rosalynd's hand tighten on my arm from behind.

Jeff had moved his lazy eyes from Matt and now they were looking at the large Mexican in front of him. He said, his voice still pitched low, "Jorge — you don't drop that knife, I'll take it from you." He was smiling, but you couldn't call it friendly. "And your thumb will feel awfully numb."

Jorge, not taking heed, crouched as Jeff drew closer and without warning sprang at him, the knife thrusting out.

Rosalynd made a noise in alarm, but Jeff didn't need the warning. He moved like lightning, catching Jorge's thrusting arm with both of his, and then abruptly spinning and repositioning, he launched the large Mexican over his shoulder. Jorge sailed nearly to where we were standing and then slammed heavily into the hard ground on his opposite shoulder. The knife skittered across the gravel, and moving fast I got to it and picked it up.

Jorge made a painful groan and tried rolling over off his shoulder, but from the odd look of it, I suspected it was dislocated. He certainly wasn't moving very well. Matt's cellar crew stood frozen, shocked by the sudden speed at which Jeff had moved and dispatched their champion, and maybe also now that I had ahold of the knife.

Jeff turned his eyes back on Matt.

Matt, who had for some reason lost his amusement over the situation, looked around desperately at his crew, but none of them wanted to get pummeled into the dirt like Jorge and weren't making any bold moves. Jeff started towards Matt again, and Matt seeing how things now stood did the only sensible thing he had left. He took off running.

Only Jeff had had to keep his fury in check this whole time and now that his prey was in easy reach he wasn't about to let Matt go, and took off after him like an angry lion.

Matt ran first for his truck, but Jeff was gaining on him, and Matt saw that that was no good so instead cut across wildly toward the paved road. Jeff, not slowing down pursued and at each dodge or change of direction Matt made, he cut the distance until he was nearly upon him. As they reached the pavement, Jeff, giving no regard to his own flesh or Matt's, dove and tackled him, slamming both down hard against the asphalt.

They rolled in a heap, and then Matt tried to scramble

desperately to his feet, but Jeff had fastened on and wasn't letting go and soon was straddling him. Matt squirmed and twisted under Jeff's grip not giving up, and even managed to elbow him in the side of the face, so Jeff raised a fist and launched a punishing blow at Matt's head.

Only Matt twisted at the last second out of the way and Jeff punished the pavement instead. The smack made by his fist hitting the ground right next to Matt's ear was so loud and hard, that for a second I thought I felt reverberations all the way to where I was standing.

Without hesitating Jeff raised his fist again for another go at Matt's head, but Matt immediately froze and gave up the fight, and it was no wonder. Anybody who could hit cold asphalt that hard without flinching could without doubt squash your head like a melon.

Jeff, holding Matt by the front of his shirt and with his fist still raised, pulled him to a sitting position and by that time we had caught up to them, Rosalynd, Álvaro and me. There was Halleran and Matt's cellar crew still to deal with, but none of them seemed to want to join in on the ruckus, so we kept an eye on them, or more like both eyes. Jeff barked angrily at Matt, "You knock those barrels down?"

Matt didn't answer right away, so Jeff raised his fist again to sock him one. "Wait!" Matt wailed. "Don't hit me!"

"We know it was you!"

Matt's eyes looked like they had sunk back in his head. He licked his lips.

"You run Chris off Spring Mountain Road?" Jeff went on,

still barking.

"No!"

"The white pickup that rammed Chris is right over there!"

Matt's eyes glanced toward the equipment shed. "It wasn't me!"

"It's your truck! It was you!"

"No. It wasn't me! I swear! It could've been anybody," he said, grasping at anything. "It — the keys! The keys are always in it! It could've been somebody else! I swear it wasn't me!"

Halleran who had joined us piped up, "Matt was here the whole time crushing grapes when Chris had his accident."

Álvaro said, "And you know all about that."

Halleran snarled, "I know Matt didn't do it!"

Jeff gave Matt another shake and growled, "You knocked those barrels down! You ran Chris off that road! And you killed Vic, didn't you?"

"No! For God's sake, no!"

"You forged that wine! That's a felony! Knocking down those barrels with an attempt to kill — another felony! Hit-and-run — felony! And cold-blooded murder of Vic Miranda! You're gonna get the electric chair!"

I noticed as Jeff ran down the list of crimes, Matt's cellar rats were quickly abandoning the sinking ship, scurrying in nearly every direction at once. Soon all that were left were Matt, Halleran and Jorge, still on the ground nearby groaning over his dislocated shoulder.

I thought it was about time we got the authorities involved

and Jeff agreed, and being busy holding onto Matt, had given Rosalynd the number to call on her cell, and soon she was talking with dispatch and telling them that off-duty Deputy Jeff Beckwell was calling for assistance, and where we were located.

Matt's face looked pale and a muscle in his neck kept twitching so it made it hard to look at him. He repeated over and over, "No! It wasn't me! It wasn't me!"

I said, "Then who was it Matt?"

You could tell he probably knew, but he didn't want to say, but there was Jeff with his fist still raised, so he finally blurted, "I couldn't let Chris tell about the wine!"

"What about the forged wine?" Jeff barked. "Tell us!"

And then the floodgates opened and everything spilled out — how Matt along with Vic and Benny and Gerry Zacks had concocted this scheme to unload some of Matt's unsold inventory at Bakerwood Winery by re-labeling it as Maverick Cellars' Reserve and then selling it abroad, mostly to the Asian markets. "It would've be a cinch with Gerry's connections in Asia," Matt spilled, "and since the Reserve would get five or six times the amount I was getting for my wines, everybody would split a fortune. Only Vic soured on the deal and wouldn't go along."

"Who killed Vic, Matt?" I asked.

Matt licked his lips again. "Vic wouldn't go through with it — he thought it would harm Maverick Cellars' reputation having my wine accepted as his," his voice turned suddenly spiteful, "which was like saying my wine was crap, and it wasn't!"

"Who tossed him in that vat?"

Matt went on, "Bakerwood was having a hard go at it and I owed — listen, I needed that money, you have no idea how much I needed that dough, and so did Gerry Zacks! He was strapped for cash too in a big way and what with him and Vic and Benny and that Goddamned vineyard property of Galbraith's. All of us had a lot riding on that deal. Zacks said he'd take care of Vic, and I thought he meant he'd go talk with him, convince him to come back in with us, but you know what happened!"

"You're saying Gerry Zacks killed Vic?"

"Who else could it be? And, and—" Matt stammered, "he could've taken the pickup! Yeah, and went after you with it, Chris!"

That was when we heard the sirens, and Matt's face kind of hollowed out. Halleran wasn't looking too good at the moment either and for a second I thought he was going to bolt like the rest of the rats, and I said it would be better on him if he stuck around, so he did.

Soon two squad cars pulled up and killed the sirens, but left the bubble lights spinning, and several deputies joined us and took Matt into custody, while Jeff filled them in on what had transpired. I noticed Jorge still sitting on the ground with his shoulder and arm hanging painfully, trying to pick up his ball cap that had fallen into the dirt and failing at it on account of his thumb obviously being too numb and not working properly. So I walked over and picked up his hat for him and placed it on his head. Then the authorities got Jorge on his feet and into a squad car.

Matt was still on the ground on his belly being cuffed by the deputies, and Jeff with Rosalynd and Álvaro were watching, when I put to Jeff, "The electric chair?"

Jeff stifled a chuckle, and said defensively, "I scared him, didn't I?"

Rosalynd said, "Jeff, you scared everybody."

He thought about that for a second and then nodded.

"So you believe him?" I asked.

"Matt?" Jeff asked back.

I nodded.

"Right now, Matt would say anything to save his own hide," Jeff said. "But he'll have to go over everything a thousand times before the boys are through with him. We'll get at the truth eventually."

More department personnel were expected to arrive any minute and more questions would be answered by everybody including Rosalynd, Álvaro, Jeff and myself, and there was also the white pickup in the shed to deal with, and the forged wine back at Maverick Cellars, which got me thinking about the wine bottles I still had in the Jeep. I had wanted to test them against a bottle of the real stuff I had stored back at my apartment, and told Jeff about it, and why I wanted to head over there right now and get it, but Jeff shook his head.

"No. First we better go to the hospital."

"The hospital?"

"Why?" Rosalynd asked.

"Because," Jeff said, "I think I broke my hand."

Chapter 19

AFTER TAKING JEFF to Queen of the Valley Hospital, and finding that he had indeed broken his hand and would be all right once the bones were reset and a cast put on, Rosalynd, Álvaro and I swung by my place with me driving Jeff's Jeep and got the Reserve bottle I had stored there and brought it back with us to Maverick Cellars along with the two bottles I had taken from the cave.

If Matt Bakerwood had been telling the truth and the wine in the Maverick Cellars caves was indeed a forgery instigated by him and the others, then that wine was most likely the motive behind Vic's death, but I had to be absolutely sure before going to the Sheriff.

So once at Maverick Cellars, Rosalynd and I left Álvaro

to explain what had happened at Bakerwood Winery to the troops and we headed for the offices. I wanted to check up on purchase orders and invoices having to do with the initial shipments of Reserve wine. I was thinking there were two possibilities. Either the wine in the caves was the forgery and not the real wine, as Matt claimed, or, the wine that had been shipped already to Maverick Cellars' customers had been Matt Bakerwood's and the wine right now in the caves was the real stuff, which would really foul things up. So telling Rosalynd what to look for we went through the files and scrounged around for about fifteen minutes, but it was wasted energy. There was nothing in the files or on anybody's desk or hidden under piles of other work, or in the trash for that matter. I couldn't even locate our customer database on the computer where all the addresses and shipping information was kept. Frankly, I hadn't really expected to find anything.

"Well, if it was here," Rosalynd said, "it's not now."

I nodded. "A safe assumption."

"But the customers who already received the wine," she went on, "surely you know of a few of them we could contact."

"I do," I said, "and we could, but there's an easier way. C'mon."

With the bottles I had brought from the Jeep, Rosalynd and I went to the back of the winery near the crush pad where the wine lab was located, and heading inside I flipped on the lights.

White-enameled worktables with stools ran along the length of one side of the room, with glass-fronted cabinets on the wall full of chemical supplies and other lab equipment, and I quickly got out what I needed to do a rough acid test on the wines using the Ripper method, and a pH test using a pH meter, not that the tests would be definitive, but they might help. I had Rosalynd collect a number of wine glasses from the cabinets and place them on the countertop and found a cork puller in one of the drawers and soon had all three bottles opened, being careful to keep them separated.

Then I poured out the wines in the glasses, three for each of us. We sat down on the stools for our own private wine tasting, only I had never tasted wine with the expressed interest in establishing a motive for murder.

"You think just by tasting you can pick out which wine is Maverick Cellars'?" Rosalynd asked slyly.

I shrugged. "It's worth a try."

So we each took up a glass and I held mine to the light to judge the clarity and color, and Rosalynd imitating me followed along. Then I swirled the wine, and Rosalynd swirled, then I put my nose over the rim and sniffed, and Rosalynd did likewise. Then we both tasted.

"No," I said, watching her, "swish it around in your mouth first. Let the esters go up into the nasal cavity."

Rosalynd took another sip and I watched as she swished it around this time.

"We taste only a few sensations," I said, "salty, sweet, sour, and bitter, along with maybe umami, but the nose can distinguish nearly ten thousand different aromas."

She nodded.

"Let's try the other ones," I said.

We did, looking first for clarity and color, and then swirling to mix the wine with oxygen to release the aromas, and then sipping and swishing.

"Well," I asked her, "can you taste the difference?"

"I don't know. They seem very similar."

I nodded. They were indeed very similar. After all, Matt Bakerwood had been trained by Vic like I had been. "Maverick Cellars' Reserve is known for its goût de terroir, its sense of place, which can often be described as a sort of chalkiness."

Rosalynd was nodding.

I went on, "It gives the wine structure and supports the fruit, which usually runs toward—"

"—blackberrys!" she said with a sense of triumph.

"That's right." I smiled. "The perfume can be very enticing, often of violets and roses, but again always with the blackberries and the chalk."

"Then this wine is the real Reserve," she said with confidence, pointing at the bottle I had brought from home. "No question about it. The other wine reminds me more of plums, or maybe cherries and it seems — I don't know —"

"Yeah, the other wine is good, no question about it. It's well made, but the Reserve comes from a great vineyard and the density and richness shines through. It's right there in the glass. Matt's a good winemaker, but Vic was a great winemaker, and I think you can taste the difference."

"I can," Rosalynd said with growing satisfaction.

"Amazing," I said back to her, and I hadn't meant just Vic's ability to make superb wine.

Rosalynd's eyes were sparkling.

Before we could go on and run some lab tests with the equipment I had gotten out, raised voices outside the lab door warned us of somebody approaching, and in a couple of seconds Eric bounded in very agitated with Benny closely following.

Eric's eyes leaped around the lab, first taking me in and then the opened wine bottles on the countertop along with the glasses, and then the lab equipment I had out, and then finally Rosalynd. From the way his face darkened at the sight of her, I thought right then and there we were into some trouble. "What in Christ's name—"

"No, not Christ — Chris," I corrected, which Eric failed to find funny at all.

"Chris, Goddamnit! What the hell're you doing?"

"Isn't it obvious? I'm testing the bogus wine we found in the caves."

"We've heard all about the caves and what you've done!"

"Then you probably also heard about what Matt Baker-wood has done, and how right now he's under arrest and in the custody of the Napa Valley Sheriff and more than likely spilling his guts."

"I'm not interested in Matt Bakerwood," Eric spat. "This is about you! And how you've put Maverick Cellars — our whole business — in jeopardy!"

"No, Eric. The forgery put Maverick Cellars in jeopardy." I looked at Benny who was still near the door. "Matt said that he, along with you, Benny, and Vic and Gerry Zacks put this whole scheme together."

Eric butted in, all but choking, "You stand there and accuse my father of being wrapped up—"

"Eric, shut up," I said, staying on Benny. "Is that true, Benny? Were you wrapped up in this forgery scheme like Matt said?"

Benny swallowed and said, "I don't know anything about any wine scheme, Chris. I swear to God." He was shaking his head for added emphasis. "I've never heard anything about any such nonsense. Matt's lying, obviously."

"Of course Matt's lying! And so are you!" Eric was glaring hotly and had taken a couple of steps towards me. I had seen that look from him before, the last time he had nearly thrown a punch, so I squared on him and set my feet and tried once more to reason with him.

"Don't you see, Eric," I said. "This scheme was probably what got your father killed."

But Eric was beyond reason. "What do you care about my father? You never cared about him—" and here came the punch. He couldn't have telegraphed it better.

So I stepped inside the swing and Eric's fist glanced off my shoulder instead of my nose, and before I realized it I was swinging in retaliation, having had about all I could stand of people trying to knock me around. My punch landed, only Eric had seen it coming and at the last instance dodged. My fist smacked into the side of his neck instead of his face, which probably saved my hand from cracking against hard skull, and

I thought how strange that a punch doesn't sound much like it does in the movies, it sort of makes a softer slapping sound if anything, even when it really connects, and mine had. The blow staggered Eric and he grabbed at me to keep his feet and our scrap turned into a wrestling match with him trying to shove me off my feet and me shoving back to keep them.

The lab got smaller, at least it felt like that as we bound around into cabinets and then tables, overturning lab stools and smashing equipment. We staggered and hopped around as dignified as a couple of drunken rabbits slapping at each other when the counter with the opened bottles of wine and glasses was struck, tumbling everything onto the floor with a horrendous crash and clatter. A bottle spouting wine soaked my pants to the skin before bouncing off the rubber floor runners and rolling under our feet. It was then that I managed to get a good shove at Eric, backing him up and then, as luck would have it, he tried to correct and in the process inadvertently stepped on one of the overturned bottles. The bottle rolled and Eric went over backwards and on the way down struck his head on a metal lab stool, taking it down with more clattering, and the fight was over.

Eric, having rung his bell thoroughly — and I knew what that was like — tried to get to his feet, but failed on his first attempt, and Benny had to get a hand under his arm to help him up.

"Let me alone!" he spat in anger. "This ain't over!"

But it was, because Benny easily backed Eric up making room for Rosalynd and I to leave the lab.

243

Benny said to me, "Go."

Eric shouted, "You're fired, Chris! You hear me? You're shit-canned, asshole!"

I looked at Benny.

But Benny just repeated, "Go."

So Rosalynd and I did, and almost immediately outside the doorway we ran into Álvaro and some of the troops.

"You are fired?" Álvaro asked with alarm.

I said, "Yep. Looks like."

Álvaro stared at me in disbelief. Then his countenance hardened. "Then I quit too," he said.

"No. You need your job. You stay put," I said, and then smiled at him, touched by his loyalty. "I'll be all right."

———

The next morning, Rosalynd and I were in a coffee shop off of Trancas in Napa, waiting for the barista to finish making our coffees. It was around ten o'clock in the morning, and though I had told Álvaro that I would be all right, I still felt out of sorts not working with him at Maverick Cellars like I usually was at this time of the morning, also realizing I would probably never be working there with him ever again.

I looked over at Rosalynd standing beside me. "You still hanging around?"

She had that amused smile of hers going.

I said, "I guess it wasn't my money you found interesting, since you're aware I'm currently jobless."

"I'm here because you promised me a croissant," she said, holding up the pastry I had gotten for her.

"And I deliver on my promises."

"I never had any doubts you wouldn't."

The barista called out my name and I went and retrieved our order, latte for Rosalynd and a double cappuccino for me, and once we had them doctored up to our liking with both sugar and cinnamon, we found an empty table and sat down.

Almost immediately, my cell rang. It was Jeff. After leaving Maverick Cellars last night, Rosalynd and I had driven back to the hospital and had taken Jeff home, and he would've been with us this morning having coffee too, but when I had called him earlier, he hadn't answered his phone.

"Hey," I said, into the cell.

"Me," he answered.

"I called you this morning. Rosalynd and I are having coffee—"

"Skip that for a moment," Jeff said, interrupting. "We found Gerry Zacks."

I looked at Rosalynd and repeated to her what Jeff had just said.

"The reason I didn't call you back is that I'm up on Mount St. Helena — at the Bubble. Seems Bridget Bordeaux was right. Gerry was out rock-climbing after all."

"You tracked him down?"

"The Department did. Chris, he's dead."

I repeated this to Rosalynd. For some reason I had half expected this to be the case all along.

Jeff went on, "He was found in his car, propped up behind

the wheel and would probably still be propped up there if a bear hadn't smelled him rotting inside and broken in the back window."

I swallowed back some bile at the thought.

Jeff continued, "Not only was Gerry's business gobbled up by a bear market, so was Gerry."

"But the bear hadn't killed him," I said.

"No. The coroner thinks he might've hit his head, or maybe was struck on the head. But it's hard to tell, especially after the bear had had his way with him. You should see this."

"I'm glad I can't," I said, and meant it. "So when did he die?"

"The coroner believes with this much decomposition, the body had to have been here for at least ten days, possibly two weeks."

"So before Vic was killed?"

"Yep." Then Jeff said, "You know what that means, don't you?"

I did. "Gerry couldn't have killed Vic."

"Yep," he said.

"And if Gerry didn't kill him, you know who did."

"Yep," Jeff said.

And so did I.

Chapter
20

ROSALYND PULLED HER convertible off onto the gravel at
the edge of the road and came to a stop. I got out and so did
she, but Rosalynd stayed at the car as we had already decided.
We were on Maverick Cellars' property and I was heading
out into the vineyard where he was sitting all by himself on
a tractor.

I walked all the way up to him, until I was standing directly
before him in front of the tractor's bucket, and the whole way
he never glanced up even once in my direction.

I said, "It was you, wasn't it?"

Benny finally looked up at me, but that was it. He didn't
say anything.

"I just heard they found Gerry Zacks," I went on.

After a long moment, Benny nodded, I wasn't sure if that was confirmation or not.

"The coroner thinks Gerry's been dead a long time, since before Vic was killed. That means there is only one person who could've pushed Vic into that vat. You, Benny."

Benny nodded again.

"Why did you do it?"

Benny didn't answer. Instead he looked out at the vineyard, and at the winery in the distance. I had almost given up that he would ever answer me when he said, "Maverick Cellars was built by both of us. We were equal partners. Fifty-fifty. Vic — he would've told you how we never would've been as successful as we ultimately were if I hadn't been his partner. I had a lot to do with Maverick Cellars' success."

"I know, Benny."

But he went on as if he hadn't heard me. "Only, nobody seemed to think so. They thought it was all Vic. Vic was the winemaker. Vic was the celebrity. Vic was Maverick Cellars. I got lost in the hoopla. Do you know how that feels?"

I nodded.

"It feels terrible. Never getting your due for all the work you've done, everything you've sacrificed. Vic had a family, had a wife, had a son and daughter, grandchildren, but I never did. I never had the time. I gave everything to Maverick Cellars. Everything. But Vic got all the credit. So when Gerry Zacks wanted to buy into Maverick Cellars, be a part of what Vic and I together had created, I saw it as the perfect opportunity to finally do something that would put me in front. Vic didn't think we needed to expand. He thought Maverick Cellars was big enough as it was, but with Gerry's money we had an opportunity to buy Galbraith's property and so I talked him into going along. We took Zacks on as a third partner and purchased the property and started extensive reinvestment in the vineyards, but that costs money and Gerry had gotten himself overextended, what with his Telecom business and all the rest, and had wanted to pull out. We hadn't even owned the property for three years and already he was pulling up roots."

Benny shook his head. "Gerry said he didn't want to pull out, it's just that the property had a rather substantial balloon payment coming due, and he couldn't make it, he was out of cash, and when we talked it over with Vic, Vic said we didn't need the property in the first place so let it go. He said 'let it go.' But I couldn't let it go. As far as I could see, it was simple really. We just needed enough money to make the balloon payment and then after that we could probably handle what we owed with what profits the vineyard could produce. I knew Matt was having trouble. He was way overextended. That winery he had built was costing him a fortune, and he had a lot of inventory that was languishing. So I thought, if we used Gerry's sources in Asia to unload Matt's wine with Maverick Cellars' label on it, well, we could make the balloon payment and Matt could pay off some of his debts and who would've complained? Not the Asians. The wine was good. So what if they thought they were buying Maverick Cellars' Reserve? I know that's callous, but I'd be willing to bet nobody over there could even tell the difference."

Benny smiled. "So we went ahead. It was easy to convince Matt. The plan eliminated two problems for him. One was all the wine he had sitting around, and the other problem was all his debts. He was easy, and so was Gerry, in the end. He didn't think we'd have any problems, because the government had already received their taxes on both wines so there was little danger of anybody finding out, and he could sure use the money. He was in bigger financial distress than Matt was. If I had known that beforehand, I might've had second thoughts — but maybe not."

Then Benny frowned. "Now there was only Vic to get on board, but he decided he didn't like the idea. Vic didn't like having bottles of wine out there with his name on the label that were not his wines, and no matter how I tried to convince him, he wouldn't budge. Finally Gerry said he'd talk with him and convince him, but Vic can be stubborn. You have no idea how stubborn. Gerry couldn't convince him, but Gerry still wanted to go along with the deal, so he proposed re-labeling the wine without Vic's consent, but what I didn't know was that Gerry no longer wanted to make the balloon payment on Galbraith's old property, he wanted to use what money we were going to make to shore up his other failing businesses. When I found that out, I didn't know what to do. I tried to talk Gerry out of it, but he could be stubborn too, so I followed him up to that rock-climbing spot. I never intended to hurt Gerry or threaten him or anything, I was just going to reason with him. Show him how it was in his best interest to keep the land. Land is always the best investment in the long run, but he wouldn't go along. He wouldn't and the next thing I knew I had this rock in my hand and Gerry was lying on the ground, and I must've hit him in the head with the rock, and he wasn't breathing too good, and I panicked. I put him in his car and thought maybe if he was found later, they would just think he had taken a spill climbing those rocks and had made it back to the car and that was it. The first couple days were brutal. You have no idea. I expected any moment for the cops to show up at Maverick Cellars and take me into custody. But then two days stretched into four, and then five and then seven, and I was starting to relax. Maybe everything might work out after all. With all the work I had done at Maverick Cellars over the years, I certainly deserved it. I thought rightly as it turned out that everyone down at Gerry's companies would just think the stress had gotten to him and he had hightailed it to China or somewhere, and I used it to my advantage. I planned to go ahead with the Asian deal, use Gerry's connections, they were already in place after all, and when they found Gerry's body, there was nothing linking it with me. Only Vic found out that we were going ahead with the deal without his consent."

"How?" I asked.

"He found the re-labeled wine. He knew like you did that we had already shipped the wine, and when he saw all those cases, he went through the roof. He said he was going to tell the Feds. I pleaded with him. I told him how much this deal meant to me, but he said we had Maverick Cellars and that

that ought to be enough. Said I was throwing away every-thing that we had built up over the years, that I couldn't be that foolish, and he turned his back on me and he went to fiddling with his stupid fermentations. But he had no idea I had already killed Gerry."

"So you tossed him into that vat."

"It was very likely everyone would think Gerry's death had been an accident, and with Vic standing there with his back to me, in an instant I realized if he went into that tank head first, everyone would think Vic had had an accident too. It was so easy, and before I thought much more about it, Vic was in the vat."

Benny smiled at me.

"I was free and now Maverick Cellars was all mine. Once I got that wine out of the caves and on a boat to Asia I'd have the property too. And there was no way for anyone to know I had done it. How could they? It was just an unfortunate winery accident. It happens from time to time, even to those who are experienced. And everyone thought so, everyone except you, Chris."

His eyes narrowed at me, and I saw him glance down at something on the tractor's dash.

Benny went on, "You wouldn't leave it alone. I thought if enough time passed, you might come around, but you kept asking questions and making a nuisance of yourself, and then that damn article in the Sentinel, and I knew I had to start keeping a better eye on you. So I started following you around, you and that deputy friend of yours."

"You were the one driving the white pickup," I said.

"You kept digging and digging, and putting it together, and after going to talk with Galbraith's kid, well, I knew I had to do something."

I saw Benny look at the dash of the tractor again, so I started moving closer to him. I said, "It was you who ran me off Spring Mountain Road."

"I had followed you up the mountain, and that road is steep and treacherous in places and I thought another perfect place for a convenient accident, so I waited for you to start back down the mountain. I knew just the spot, where the road took a bend and fell away sharply. If I managed to catch you just right you'd go over and that would be the end of that. And that's just what happened. Only you didn't die."

I saw Benny look down at the dash again, and this time, I had moved up close enough to catch sight of what it was he was looking at. It was the tractor's ignition, so I moved forward before he managed to get his hands on the key to start the tractor, and I pulled the key out. I didn't need him entertaining the thought he might just get out of his current jam by having me suffer a tractor accident.

That was when we both heard the sirens. Benny looked up and I turned to glance back at the road and there they came, three squad cars from the Sheriff's Department, and they pulled over nearly where Rosalynd was waiting. When the first car came to a halt, and the door opened, I saw immediately it was Coulette himself who had arrived to take Benny into custody.

—∞—

It was a little after one in the afternoon as Rosalynd and I headed up Valley on the Silverado Trail from her place in Stag's Leap to my place in St. Helena. Rosalynd was driving her Mercedes and the top was up, and I was looking out the window at the vineyards that line the road. The day had turned colder than expected and the sky was threatening rain, though it hadn't started yet, and the clouds above were dark and turbulent as they crossed the sky, sort of broken up into clumps so the sun could still peek through now and again to shine down onto the landscape. The grape leaves in the vineyards were already starting to change, taking on the varying hues of gold and red, and with the sunlight shining down upon them the Napa Valley never looked more splendid. I wasn't the only one who thought so, because every car it seemed that happened down the road at that moment that also happened to have a camera inside was pulling over to the side and people were getting out to snap some pictures, because nearly everywhere you turned your head was a view worthy of a thousand photographs.

Right then Napa Valley was perhaps the most beautiful place on the planet, and I couldn't help thinking about Vic and the life that he had lived here, and the choices he had made. It had been a good life, and he had been a good man, and a good friend, and he had lived his life to the fullest. I knew he would have thought so too.

Once we got to my apartment, neither of us felt like going out again to get something to eat, so I thought we might hunt through the cupboards and see if I had enough around to whip something together. Since the day was cold, I thought we might need something to warm us up, and I found a tin of smoked trout and an onion that wasn't too ripe, and some canned chicken broth and then dug out some Arborio and a small block of Parmigiano Reggiano that I kept in the fridge.

"How about risotto?"

Rosalynd agreed, and I told her where to find a bottle of Chenin Blanc I had that would be perfect with it, and we set it to chill in the fridge, while I chopped the onion. Rosalynd sat back at the kitchen table to watch as I got the pan on the stove and with a little butter got the onions to sauté gently. It's best to cook onions slowly, to bring out the best flavor, and neither of us had anywhere to go, or so I thought, so I took my time, using a wooden spoon to keep the onions moving in the pan and caramelizing nicely. Once the onions were the way I liked them, I tossed in the rice and let the browned butter coat the grains well, and then got out the bottle of Chenin Blanc from the fridge and poured in about a cup. Once the rice had absorbed the wine, I began to add some of the chicken broth a little at a time, stirring gently until the rice incorporated all the liquid and the creamy sauce from the rice began to form. When the grains had softened to my satisfaction, I took the pan off the heat and got the tin of smoked trout and broke chunks of the fish into the rice stirring it in gently and then adding a little of the oil from the tin. At the last, I grated some cheese over the dish and stirred it in too, and then it was time to eat. I got a couple of bowls for the rice and half a baguette from the freezer that took about a minute to defrost in the toaster, and with a couple of glasses of the old vine Chenin, we had a meal.

Rosalynd got a forkful of rice, which was still steaming and blew on it until it was cool enough to taste and did so and then looked over at me sharply. "You *are* a gourmet."

"Maybe I was showing off a little."

"This is delicious."

I agreed. The old vine Chenin Blanc was pretty good too, but before I could get much of it down we were interrupted when somebody started banging on my front door.

I got up to look. It was Marjorie, and I could see that she could see me now too through the glass and was smiling and waving.

"It's my landlady, Marjorie," I said to Rosalynd who was also getting up to see who it was. "She seems to be a little upset."

I went ahead and opened the door, swinging it wide but before I could even say, 'hello', Marjorie rushed past.

"Oh, Chris. Thank God I caught you home. You have to come right away. The lizard is back!" That last bit Marjorie all but shrieked.

Her distress was on account of the lizard again — the lizard that I had failed to catch for her in the first place. The lizard I had also failed to tell her I hadn't caught in the first place because Marjorie had had the habit of not letting me get a word in edgewise. "About the lizard—" I started, but Marjorie of course interrupted.

"You have to come right away. I can't stand it!"

"All — all right," I finally managed to edge in. "I'm coming."

"Oh, good!" Marjorie smiled then at Rosalynd.

I asked her if she had met Rosalynd before and I learned they had met at the hospital when I was recovering, so having that settled all three of us headed to Marjorie's. As I let them precede me through the door, Marjorie turned back suddenly and whispered so Rosalynd wouldn't overhear, "Rosalynd's a real beauty, isn't she?"

I certainly thought so, so I nodded. Marjorie then gave me a playful pinch, and smiling, caught up quickly with Rosalynd. I followed them toward the house. As we reached the back porch, Jeff hollered at us from across the yard in his Jeep, waving at us with his cast.

I said, "C'mon, you're just in time to help me catch a lizard."

Jeff quickly caught up and this time the lizard wasn't in the kitchen under a plastic container, but in the front room under the couch.

Marjorie explained, "I said that the lizard was back, but that's not exactly true, because this lizard is much bigger."

"Bigger?" Rosalynd asked suddenly alarmed.

"Uh-huh. More like a snake with legs!"

"A snake!" Rosalynd nearly shrieked.

"I saw it slither quickly across the carpet and dive under."

Both Marjorie and Rosalynd were keeping their distance as Jeff and I advanced on the couch.

"I bet it's nearly a foot long," Marjorie went on in horror.

"Much bigger that the one Chris caught for me."

"About the lizard I caught," I said. "I didn't catch it." Before Marjorie could interrupt, I held up a palm. "What I caught under the container was a pencil."

"A pencil!" Marjorie exclaimed, and then when it finally sunk in enough she started to laugh. "Oh, I'm so embarrassed. Was it really a pencil?"

"Yep," I said.

"Oh, you must think I'm losing my mind!"

I smiled and looked at Jeff. We were in position. "This is the plan," I said. "I'll lift my end of the couch and move it quickly to the side, and if you see the lizard coming your way, grab it."

"Got it," Jeff said.

I grabbed the couch and swung it away from the wall and immediately, we saw the lizard. Both Marjorie and Rosalynd shrieked at the sight of it, which didn't help matters any, and the lizard bolted my way instead of Jeff's so I had to quickly drop the couch and pounce. And I got it.

Jeff said, "Let me see. Let me see."

So I opened my hand enough for the lizard to poke his head out. It wasn't a foot long snake with legs. Actually, it was barely three inches.

"There he is," Jeff cooed. "Oh, let me hold him."

I carefully handed the lizard to Jeff, who got it to rest on the palm of his cast by gently stroking it. "Look at him. Would you just look at the little fella?" We all did as Jeff asked, even Marjorie and Rosalynd, though if Jeff had made any sudden moves I suspected both would've bolted from the room. Jeff turned the lizard over carefully to peek at the underside, and then said, "I was wrong. He's a she. Yep, he's a she."

Rosalynd was dubious. "How can you tell if it's a he or a she?"

"See this little fold," Jeff pointed. "That's the cloaca, that's how I know."

Rosalynd was still dubious.

"I believe he's right," I said to her.

"Oh, you do?" she said to me. Was she now suspicious of me too?

"Of course I'm right," Jeff said, as if he couldn't understand why anybody would ever doubt him.

Marjorie pointed and said, "I don't care what gender the lizard is, just put him — I mean her — outside."

Jeff did as Marjorie ordered and put the lizard in the garden. Then he looked at Rosalynd, all of us having followed him outside and asked, "Did you tell him?"

She said, "No. Not yet."

When, I thought, had they had any time to confer when I hadn't been there to hear it? "Tell me what?" I asked.

"Well," Rosalynd said, "D.H. is back from the East Coast, and he wondered if you'd do him a favor."

"Absolutely. Anything," I said. Then I asked, "How long was he on the East Coast anyway?"

"About eleven hours," she said. "He hopped a flight right back. Got in late last night."

"So what's the favor?"

The favor as it turned out was a piece of property in the Los Carneros region of Napa Valley that D.H. wanted to hear my appraisal of once I got a chance to look at it, so that's where Rosalynd, Jeff and I would head once we finished lunch.

There was plenty of risotto and wine so Jeff joined us. We asked Marjorie to join us too, but she was meeting with her guy friend again so declined our invitation. Before she split, though, she had to tell us all about their first date.

"I've mentioned to you how he likes to talk," she said, rolling her eyes, "And talk, and talk, and talk. Well, of course I tuned him out after five minutes and proceeded to get thoroughly crocked! I did! When finally I had to butt in and ask, 'When're you going to ask me anything about me? Aren't you even curious?' So he asked about what I liked to do, and I told him about my dance group and about my collection of antique furniture, and then he said, 'I've never seen an antique that couldn't be improved with a box of matches.'"

"Ouch," I said.

"You poor thing," Rosalynd empathized.

"Can you believe that?" Marjorie's eyes flared. "I would've doused him with my drink, if I hadn't already finished it."

Then Jeff asked the obvious question, "So why in pity's sake are you meeting with this guy again?"

"Because, silly," she said with a naughty grin. "I told you before how good looking he is." And with that she laughed and in moments was in her car and gone.

The property that D.H. wanted us to visit was south of Napa, in that rolling countryside influenced so strongly by the proximity to San Pablo Bay.

When we arrived the property turned out to be a vine-yard and winery on a little over ten acres, and I understood immediately, or so I thought, what D.H. had wanted. He was leaning on his Ferrari with his cell pressed to his ear, so we angled in next to him in Rosalynd's car, and she abruptly shut off the engine. We got out and D.H. still busy on the phone waved us towards the property to have a look around while he finished chatting, and he would catch up in a sec. So we walked out into the vineyard planted to Pinot Noir, and I could see at once that it had been severely neglected. The vineyard was old, probably forty-five to fifty years if I had to guess, with many missing plants and more than a few suffer-ing from viruses and or dying. It would have to be thoroughly replanted.

Having seen enough, we headed for the winery and crush pad. I had thought I had had to work with old equipment at Maverick Cellars, but this place made Maverick Cellars look like Mission Control. The tanks weren't even stainless steel, but redwood, and the barrels were mostly old, or at least I couldn't see where they had stacked the newer stuff. The tanks had wine in them from this year's harvest, and I turned the spigot and let some drip into my palm and gave it a slurp. Not good. Something was definitely off. Rosalynd and Jeff wanted to taste, even after I warned them.

After doing so, Rosalynd responded, "Ew."

"Carburetor cleaner?" Jeff queried.

"I was thinking, paint thinner, with a little cherry cola

261

mixed in."

I satisfied myself with the workings of the facility, checking the waste disposal and pond, and the electrical system, which worked, but I wasn't confident it would continue to do so if I maybe turned my back on it. We then headed outside and towards D.H. who was finishing up his call.

"So what do you think?" he asked.

"I'm not going to soft-pedal it," I said. "The vineyard is in pretty poor shape. It needs to be thoroughly replanted, and with the newer clones. The winery on the other hand — let me put it this way. I didn't know people were still making wine using equipment from the eighteen century. The wine already in tanks is off. I'm not entirely sure at this point what's wrong with it so would need a thorough analysis done. If you want to save it and not just sell it off as bulk or pour it out, that will have to be done immediately. All in all, to get this place up and running will take a lot of work — a lot of back-breaking labor. Oh, and not a small amount of money. Did I mention how much work needs to be done? A lot. I can't emphasize that enough."

As I talked, D.H. kept smiling and nodding, and saying, "Great! Good! Yep! Great!" When finally, he said, "Perfect!" And I wasn't sure he had heard me. I looked helplessly at Rosalynd and Jeff.

"If you're planning to buy this property—" I resumed.

When D.H. said, "I already have!" He had a twinkle in his eyes. "Remember that deer hoof I got with you the other day?"

"How could I forget?"

"Well, I've been working on a shoe design. When deer walk through the woods they hardly make any noise. So I thought, what if the sole on your shoe was the same shape? Only we couldn't get it exactly right without a real deer hoof to copy." Then he grinned. "I just sold the design to Sandstone Shoes for two point five million. They're calling it *The Deer Trekker!*"

I gawked.

I glanced at Jeff and Rosalynd. They were gawking too, and D.H. just laughed.

Then he said as if we doubted him, "Oh, yeah. Yeah — two point five million! That's how I'm buying this place." He swept his arm to take in the whole property. "As for all the work, from what I've seen of you and how you handle yourself, I can't think of anybody better. So hop to it!"

Jeff and Rosalynd were smiling at me, and I realized then that this was what they had secretly discussed. They knew D.H. was about to offer me a job.

"That's if you want to be my winemaker," D.H. said.

"I can't think of anybody better," I said.

"Great!" When the cell in his shirt pocket buzzed. D.H. fished it out, looked at the caller and then looked at me mischievously. "It's the girl we took the package to. Should I answer it?"

"Oh, you have to take the call," I said.

"Yeah," D.H. agreed. "Yeah. Have to."